I0680190

I DID IT MY WAY

MARK WOLODKOWICZ

Written by:
Mark Wolodkowicz
mark@jarofdreams.com

Translated by: Ksawery J. Swiecki

Edited by: Karen Majewski, Jodi Pyle &
Julie Ellis

I DID IT MY WAY

Monsieur Polskowicz
-Memoirs of an immigrant

MOCY PUBLISHING, LLC

Detroit, Michigan

I DID IT MY WAY
ISBN 978-0-9834700-8-3
Copyright © 2013 by Mark Wolodkowicz

Published by Mocy Publishing, LLC.
Website: www.mocypublishing.com
Email: info@mocypublishing.com
Phone: (313) 436-6944

All rights reserved. Except as permitted under
the United States Copyright Act of 1976, no part
of this publication may be reproduced or
distributed in any form or by any means, or
stored in a data base or retrieval system, without
the prior written permission of the publisher.

Contents:

From the Author

The book you are about to read is only partially fiction. Names of the characters are indeed product of my imagination but the course of events presented is consistent with the story of my life.

I do not consider this book to be an autobiography, though. First of all – who am I? - Certainly not someone who considers himself to be a celebrity, or somebody attempting to intrigue thousands of readers awaiting more news about my life. On the other hand, however, I am sure that situations and life circumstances, which came across my way, are far from being stereotypical. Throughout the years of my life as an immigrant I have had an opportunity to compare various ways of lives led by various generations of people. My family and professional life may seem typical and lame but only at first glance. In fact we experience the same type of disappointments whenever our values seem to lose meaning in this – like it or not – somewhat lost and chaotic world.

I also am not up for being political or suggesting political views and orientations. All of the comments you are about to find are my own personal perspective.

The main purpose I set for myself while writing this book was to expose problems we all experience on a daily basis - disintegration of families, problems with the youths, increased/overrated value of money.

Meanwhile, the romantic element of the book should equip us with some encouragement. Like it or not Love is what allows us to look

with optimism towards the future. It enriches
our intellect and shapes our sensitivity.
If you, Dear Reader, can identify yourself at
least to some extent with some of my book's
characters, my goal has been accomplished.

~Mark Wolodkowicz

Introduction

I traveled the country on Eagle's wings
- They shade half of the sky.
It's the land of candies and oranges
That the children are not meant to have.
But its people is proud
The pride drives their lives
And it's only the moments, the midst
of hunger and crime when
The drive's glamour fades away.
It is this land where my life begun.
It is this land where it will end.
For there's neither gleaming nor shadow left
there for me
Hollowed through to the bone by debt – I
remain

Chapter I

Springtime in Bydgoszcz has been always long awaited by everyone. Blooming of flowers and trees gave the fresh look to the city. Trams and buses washed and cleaned for the season, quickly running through town resembled ants transporting priceless food to their kingdom. Old SPICHRZE overlooking Brda river whispered: cold winter nights are over. It's time to take a break from drowsy thoughts and look up to the Sun with brand new energy that allows to look forward towards summer. Weeping willows behind the orchestra hall seemed to be far from weeping. Quite the opposite: rocked by gentle wind they were inviting couples in love to spend even just a second in their kind company.

On the outskirts of town behind the soccer field of "Zawisza" team two boy ages – perhaps 18 or so – marched with visible confidence towards town. By their walk you could tell that they were somewhat athletic. Equally tall their blue eyes shined from underneath blond hair. No doubts – they're brothers.

- For what in the hell did you talk me out from going to school, Andrzej?
- Don't be boring. What, do you regret?
- No, I liked it but what when mom finds out?
- Shut up, silly. She doesn't have to know.
- What if they call from school?

- They're not gonna do that over one day. Quit worrying, look there is the tram. Let's go.
- Andrzej stop. We don't have any money to get tickets.
- Geez, you're something else. We'll bum a ride.
- What if we get caught?
- Oh my! Just get in and quit being so scared and asking all these "what if?"

They were on the way to the "Wyzyny" neighborhood. They moved there from a small apartment downtown. Their father, Leon Polskowicz ran paper Company. Mother was an accountant at one of city's businesses. Both brothers were high school students.

- Finally! You're back. I was starting to worry. How was school?
- All right, mom. Tomorrow s May 1st parade so it was pretty low-key atmosphere today. Right Mark?
- Sure.
- You know what, mom? They told me at school that I would be carrying Lenin poster during the parade. I asked them "why?" and they said it was a punishment.
- Good. Carry Lenin on since you skip school so much.

- That's not what it was about. Why do they keep telling us what a great system socialism is and then tell you it's a punishment to carry poster of the leader?
- Don't start getting political with me. You know how I feel about things.
- I know but is there any solution to this situation?
- Ask your father.
- He's coming back late. I'm going to study.
- Oh, would you quit lying to your mother like that? "Study" – sure.
- Seriously. Krzysio and I will work on school stuff together. Mark, come here for a sec.
- What do you want?
- Give me a twenty.
- What? Again beer money!
- No, it's for coffee.
- Stop lying; you'll end up at "Medyk's" or at "Colors" or some other pub with all your little girlfriends.
- Is it my fault that I love them all?
- Bull, you don't love them. Their tits – maybe.
- Maybe you're right. But tits – I love them most.
- Get out of here. Just go now!

"Medyk" was a pub located in the old part of town, at Zaulek Street. In spite of its suggestive name it wasn't frequented by medical professionals as much as it was by youth, serving as their gathering spot. In partially darkened basement one could see couples in love sitting at oak tables, girls chatting and boys talking sports over a game of cards. It was also favorite place for inspiring artists and – of course – KANCIARZ trying to trade dollars for zlotys. The atmosphere of the place was inviting young talents to present their skills. It was the world created by and for the youth. One could talk about anything and everything without being afraid of potential consequences. Many of the patrons later in life were becoming quite the successful athletes, doctors, lawyers, business people, etc. The end of the 70s' favored the revival of beautiful Polish traditions. Young people were hungry for examples and role models from the past with whom to identify.

- Hi, Andrzej!
- What's up?
- Where's your brother?
- I don't think he's coming today. Why?
- I wrote a small piece of pantomime and thought he could help me with some music to it.
- I can do it.
- Come on! You know he can play better. Besides – you don't have the time.

11

- Why do you say that?
- I heard the guys downstairs talking about going to Berlin. They want you to go with them.
- I sure would. Have you seen Barb lately?
- She is downstairs.
- Hi Basia!
- Hi and bye.
- What's your problem?
- You said you would call. We were supposed to go to the theatre but you instead decided to get some beer with your cohorts from "The Colors". No time left, huh?
- That's not true. We really had a lot of business to take care of.
- Such as…?
- We met a guy who brought counterfeit stamps and medical slips so that we can get excused from classes.
- One day you will pay for this, I'm telling you, and I don't want to know anything about it.
- Get a beer, Barb. I'll be back in five minutes or so. I just need to talk this Berlin trip over with the guys.
- Berlin, again? Have you really lost your mind?

- Hey, I can make some cash so why not?
- Andrzej, finally you're here. How long you wanted me to wait?
- OK, so are we going?
- Yes,
- We're leaving on Wednesday and come back Monday. We take some stuff and bring back shoes.
- How do we get there?
- With the "Maluch" all four of us.
- Four of us packed in Fiat 126p? How are we supposed to breathe?
- Quit whining. It'll all work out.
- Fine, I'm going. I'll get back to Basia now, guys. OK?
- Take here to the party with us, at the "Kapusciska".
- Good deal. Give me the address and we'll join you.

Mark was on an overloaded bus going without paying attention to what was around him. He just finished reading "Quo Vadis" and the whole story of Vinnitius and Ligia was stuck on his mind. What an example of value of love that leads to wonders. He looked for stories with characters representing values he cared for and wanted to live by. Maybe he already had them in him but did not realize it. He knew, once he fell in love it would be the true, the real one from which he would be proud, for which he would sacrifice time and energy.

- Good evening. Mirka home?
- She'll be back shortly. Come on in, Mark. You can wait for her and her father would like to speak with you.
- Hi, Mark. Sit down and tell me what do you think about the whole "Solidarity" situation? Do you think there will be riots?
- Well, it's hard to say but if it came to defending against the Soviets – we'll defend us.
- But the Soviets – they have so much military here!
- Yes, but mind you – this is our country and nobody will threaten us with taking it over. I know history likes to repeat itself and therefore I would put my life on the line for our freedom. Life without it has no meaning.
- You've got quite the attitude considering your age.
- You know, my father was born in Vilna before WWII. The whole family lived a good and comfortable life. We had a house, the land, a store. We lived well with the Lithuanians. So when the war ended and the Russians took

14

everything nobody was happy – neither the Lithuanians nor the Poles. The only thing that was left were the wounds and disappointment. Nobody can separate mother from her children and even though they may be apart now, their hearts beat with the same rhythm in the same pace.

- Nicely put, Mark. It sounds very romantic too.

- Of course it sounds romantic because this is how we all are. I'm very proud of the fact that I can love selflessly, not for profit, not for success but just for the sake of loving something that deserves it. Fatherland has always been and always will be ours and will never betray us. Maybe you can give up a wife, but never your mother, sir. You know, sometimes I have this thought to just jump on a horse, pick up a sword and just ride through forests and meadows, and feel the scent of my land; its trees, its wheat, to love my neighbors and live in harmony. The reward and satisfaction will come on its own.

- Wow, Mark. You talk like a true nobility member. You

know, it quite impresses me
and I honestly hope you will
stay this way.
- Thanks for the complement.
- Oh, there's Mirka back. You
probably want to go now.
- Yes, we'll leave. How are
you, Mirka? Good night sir.
- Hi, Mark. Where shall we go?
- Let's just take a walk.
- Sounds good.

- What do we have to drink?
- The pure one and the
JARZEBIAK.
- Let's give it a shot
- Andrzej, play us something on
the guitar.
- Like what?
- Anything, as long as we all
have fun.
- "Wine! Oh, give me some
wine. And if I shall die, burry
me in my Ukraine, right next
to my beloved. Hey, hey the
SOKOLY." – the music kept
on going.
- He's pretty good, huh?
- Yeah, I sometimes think he
really should try at the music
school.
- Well, Basia. You know he is
one of those restless ones,
constantly flying around
somewhere.
- How is he doing at school?

16

- So – so. Sometimes he skips it for weeks. Then he comes back just to take the test and "A"s them all.
- I don't get it.
- Typical college attitude.
- Yes, but if he continues like this he will never get into college.
- Last summer he worked some public works. He didn't want to take money from his parents. You know what he used to do?
- No, what's that.
- He would steal roses and bushes and sell them under the table making double the money. Finally they caught him and fired instantly. So afterwards he went to a mill and found two dumb morons who believed him when he said he was a student in training. They were doing all the work for him while he was lying around counting dew. Ultimately they fired him too. He's always claimed to belong to free labor market, which is why in socialism he's never been appreciated. I have to give him credit though; he always has some money and an abundance of ideas how to make it.

17

- Basia, come on over here and stop talking so much.
- Give me a sec!
- Who is it there sitting with you? Hi!
- My name is Ilona, hi!
- I'm Andrzej.
- Yes, I know.
- Then I can say we've know each other for ages and if that's true then there would be nothing wrong with me inviting you to tomorrows May 1st party.
- What would Basia say?
- I'm asking you, not Basia.
- OK, I'll go. What time should we meet?
- 5-ish, next to "Kaskada".

It was 2 am when the party finally ended. Everybody slightly tipsy and tired headed towards their homes. Andrzej took the tram and was happy to get to know the new girl, Ilona. Blond" – he thought. Basia is a brunette – maybe its time for a change? They say you cannot trust the brunettes. This was his fourth girlfriend within the last three months. For a while he couldn't believe he actually forgot the name of his first two girlfriends. He didn't dwell on it though and concluded: "that's what was meant to happen".

- May 1st is tomorrow and I have to carry the Lenin and God knows why. That's

18

> unfair. It'll get better after the
> parade. We'll see what the
> guys will come up with;
> hopefully there will be no
> fights this time. Last year
> they broke my finger.

It was 3 am when he finally got home.

May 1st! Ironically the beginning of the real
spring, first warm and sunny days were to be
associated with the communist labor holiday.
Most of the people never took this day
seriously and the real reason for joy was that
it was a day off work. Young people knew
also that after the parade they could go to the
outskirts of town and party. Us Poles, as
opposed to other nations, do not care for
orders and particularly for mandatory
celebrations. Throughout years of partitions
and occupation variety of restrictions and
rules were introduced and Poles felt great joy
from breaking them. I guess it is in our blood
that whatever is forced upon is also never
respected. I don't know if one can be proud
of it but this is the reality and one has to learn
to live in it. Anniversary of the May 3rd
Constitution would certainly be respected
more, just like the one of November Uprising
or the Warsaw Uprising, etc.

Mark was parading with no particular
enthusiasm chatting with his buddy,
Grzegorz. The future was the theme of the
conversation. It was the time of very hard
decisions. The anticommunist sentiments
were on the rise while the state budget stayed

19

empty. Rationing of food, cigarettes and alcohol only fulfilled the general sense of hurt present among the people. Usually optimistic youth had a hard time compromising the contradicting feelings.

- You know what, Grzegorz, after graduation I will take up zoo-technology or agriculture. The state farms are on the verge of bankruptcy and ultimately there will be nothing left, no food-no cooking.
- Do what you have to do, Mark. I am going to enroll at KUL. I still believe that religion is the strongest engine of order and respect in this country. Besides, studying at catholic University will prevent me from being fooled by all those communistic indoctrination, which only make sense on a piece of paper.
- You know, this is what really gets me upset; when the war started we were the only ones to stand up against the Germans hoping for support. The Soviets got us from another side of the country and the support never came. The war ended. We won and look what the hell is going on. Germany got back on its feet

and they laugh at us. All around you can read; "Great nation of Poland wants to separate itself from communism". And who was it that sold us to the Soviets? So now the West claims it grants us all the loans so that we can survive. They can shove them up their butts, as far as I'm concerned. I think we ought to part from all of our "friends" and get back on our own feet; rebuild the economy and run ourselves by ourselves. I know this day will come and Poland will come back – strong and independent.

- Hey, Mark stop talking like this. You start to sound like Pilsudski.
- Grzegorz, believe me – I would give a lot to have Pilsudski here with us now.
- Look to the right, Mark! There is Andrzej with Lenin. Oh, my – that is something else!

- Danka, carry it for a minute
- You're joking, right? You asked for it yourself.
- I didn't ask for it. It's some punishment.

- Yes, since you refuse to go to school!
- Maybe I skip, but I still know what I'm supposed to know.
- You know, Andrzej, I really think there is something about you that you carefully cover up.
- Like what?
- Kindness and sensitivity.
- Quit it, Danka. Me – kind and sensitive?
- I think so, Andrzej.
- Why don't we change the subject?
- What have you been read lately?
- "Sport Review", ha, ha, ha!
- Oh, come on. I'm asking seriously.
- The history of Alexander the Great.
- For real?
- Yes, and you know what I like the most about his life story?
- What is it?
- Name of is wife; Sandra.
- Oh, Andrzej, you only have women on your mind, don't you?
- You're right, but don't you think women deserve to be interested with? This is how the world works.
- All right, all right. On the other hand I envy you.

- Why?
- Your sense of peace and the attitude marked by almost lightness of heart, the easiness with which you approach people and get to know them.
- I can teach you this, if you want. You just would have to spend more time with me.
- What do you mean by that?
- Pop in to my place tomorrow evening and I'll explain that to you.
- Are you asking me out on a date?
- No, I'm just offering you a chance.
- OK, I'll come around 8 p.m.

Reminder of the walk they spent in silence. It was just Andrzej quietly humming his favorite song: "You said you liked me because I'm like the one from a story, one who wants something; be it summer or spring. So, you didn't think about how bad I wanted to hold your hand, you didn't think of me as a clown who's so far away from it..." And he thought – "Danka want to be mine, and maybe she will be. But that's tomorrow. Today at 5 p.m. is Ilona's time, and that's what matters.

Mark was with Mirka on the tram till its last stop. Behind the railroad bridge was a forest – a very popular place for walks. The paths were filled with colorful crowd mingling in between green walls of trees and bushes. The view was like perfect harmony. Every human being is a part of nature and participates in the never-ending cycle of its life, whether knowingly or not.

How different we all are! Everyone in the secret corridors of their dreams makes plans for their future. There are some who like to talk their dreams out. Then there are those who are quite the opposite – keep them just for themselves. Has anyone wondered about the story told by the forests? Do the trees have heir own secret dreams as well…?

Mark felt like he was listening to the whispering of the trees – some of them with pride, others with sadness.

- Mirka, do you know how they say that trees die while standing?
- Yes.
- Don't you think it's kind of depressing?
- No, why?
- A standing tree should represent life not death.
- I agree, but do people die alive? I mean, a tree is like a human being – doesn't get to pick where it's planted. Once it's there it tries to use its ground as much as possible; to grow up, to become strong and the one that gives shelter and food. Same thing with

people; it is our instinct that gets us through life, to become wiser and stronger. But what is it with you? – Where all these questions from?

- Honestly I tell you; I just don't know whom will I become in the future? Graduation is right around the corner and then what? I talk to the guys, all of whom have some plans laid out for the future. One wants to do this, the other one that, and what about me? I keep lying that I know while in fact I have no clue.

- Don't ask me for an answer. I myself am clueless.

- Just because someone has plans and it looks all serious and sincere doesn't make it doable. Sometimes young tree starts to grow fast and then all of the sudden dries out. Then there is the one that is old and rotten, yet after the years becomes to live again. Let's say Poland is our land from which we take in order to live. What will happen when we use it all up?

- Mark, Mark, don't compare yourself to a tree. This is why you go to school and study – to use things wisely and once

you grow up you will fill the
land back. Isn't it simple?
- My little Mirka, you have a
quick answer to everything,
don't you? You better tell me
about your vacation plans.
- I think I'll go somewhere with
my parents but I still don't
know where to. What about
you?
- Andrzej keeps mentioning
about taking a trip by the sea.
You know how he is though –
all the details will pop out a
day before taking off.
- Your brother is something
else, isn't he?
- Everybody says so. He is
strange. I see it.
- Well, all the girls chasing him
would disagree.
- Maybe that's exactly what he
wants. But, whatever – are we
going on or shall we return?
- Let's go back.

- Hi, Andrzej!
- What's going on? You know
what time it is?
- 5:30.
- That's right, and what time
did you say you would be
here?
- The bus was late.
- Aha, well good thing I was
late myself. I wouldn't be

waiting. You want to go to
Myslecinek for a party?
- Hey, wait for me!
- Andrzej, who is it?
- Rysiu - a friend of mine.
- Hi guys, do you mind if I go
  with you?
- No problem. Where is your
  girl though?
- On a supermarket shelf – her
  name is "Zytnia" high proof.
- Well, go and get here fast.
  The tram is about to come.
- What's taking him so long?
  Look, here is the tram.
- Here he is coming right now.
- Rysiek, hurry up! The tram is
  about to leave!
- I'm coming right now!

As he was rushing, he tripped and fell. "Oh
no!" – he screamed while falling down.

- Crap! Look, Ilona – he did
  himself good. I hope he didn't
  mess himself up to bad. I
  don't think so though – he's
  picking himself up. Hurry!
  Hurry!

The three of them got on the tram.

- What were you doing, Mr.
  Acrobat!?
- Damn, I didn't see that. The
  sidewalk was crooked or
  something. But see? – I saved
  the bottle!

- Lucky you, otherwise you
  would sit dry all evening long,
  you moron.

When they arrived the square was already
filled up with young people and music was
coming from all around. Some danced while
others just chatted standing. Some couples
were busy making out on nearby benches.

- Ilona, let's dance. Rysio take
  seats for us on the bench.
- Andrzej, this is my favorite
  new piece.
- I like it too. I think "Budka
  Suflera" is the best band.

Andrzej held her passionately and the two
danced to the rhythm of the beat. Andrzej
hummed: "I failed in life again..."
Afterwards they came up to Rysiek.

- Perfect spot you picked! Give
  me a beer.
- You guys want a sip of
  "Zyto"?
- All right, I'll have a little bit.
- So Andrzej, what are we
  doing during vacation?
- Well hop in to Mielno, right
  by the sea.
- Maybe we could go
  somewhere else this time?
- I like it there. You do
  whatever you wanna do.
- Don't get pissy. You know
  we all like you a lot and will
  go with you together
  wherever.

- That's right – "with you".
  Don't you guys have your
  own ideas?
- We do but it's always fun with
  you. Remember when after
  the party at "Pojezierze" you
  started playing on fire
  hydrant?

Everybody laughed.

- Of course I remember. Those
  were the days, huh?
- What was it, Andrzej? Tell
  me! – Ilona asked.
- We went to a party at a resort
  hotel. We had great time until
  the tape recorder flopped. So,
  the manager shows up and he
  goes: "Sorry, but this is the
  only stereo we have. I'm
  afraid the party is over unless
  you guys have some idea".
  So, I'm going: "I've got one".
  He asked what? I go up to the
  fire hydrant and open it. The
  foam was everywhere while
  I'm working around with it
  singing the piece about two
  small puppies. People started
  to clap but at the end I was
  kicked out of there. Ilona,
  come on – let's dance some
  more.
- All right then.

Time was flying by fast. Some couples
started to head back towards town. Two guys

approached the bench where Rysio was
sitting.

- How are you?
- Not bad. How' bout yourself?
- What are you doing sitting on
  our bench?
- "Our bench"? Who said it
  was your bench?
- I'm saying so. Now get out of
  here.
- Wow, wow, wow…hold on
  now.

Before he was able to finish a strong punch
got him in the face. He fell on the ground.
He tried to pick himself up when the second
punch did him completely. He diodn't know
where he was or what has just happen.

- What are you waiting for?
  Get the buzz and check how
  much cash he has. – said one
  of the attackers.

Just as the were getting to flee the scene an
unexpected punch got one of them on the
ground. It was Andrzej standing right in
front of them.

- What did you do to my friend,
  asshole?
- Nothing, he got drunk and fell
  asleep.
- Is this why his nose is
  bleeding?
- I don't know what happened
  to him.
- Well, how about I remind
  you… - Andrzej was quickly

coming up towards the
stranger thug.
- OK, Ok, here is his dew and
buzz. I'm getting lost, all
right?
- Not so quickly.

He grabbed the thug by his shirt and tossed
him around while firing a powerful punch
right in his nose.
- Oh, God! – the stranger
screamed from the ground
holding his hands at his face.
They were covered in blood.
- One more time I see you and it
will be your last. Got it?
- I get it! I get it!
- Ilona come on; help me get
Rysio on his feet. Let's go
back home.

Family – sounds so simple, doesn't it? But
how much joy and… danger hides behind
this simple word and all the ups and downs.
There are those mixed feelings when we here
politicians claim that this or that was
introduced to benefit families, that such and
such policy was passed for the same purpose.
Isn't it true, though, that throughout the ages
we ourselves shaped the model of family
that's suitable? Isn't it true that family is a
responsibility of its members primarily? So
why is it that talking about it became so
fashionable ion the world of politics and
business? Leave the families alone! There is
nothing more valuable than stories of parents
about grandparents and great grandparents.

Some of them got their fame on battlefields while others gained respect through hard work and their love for people. Our future does not depend on promises. It is the sense of honor, patriotism, and love for the country that is the assurance of future successes.

- Where are the guys?
- They're still partying. They should be back soon though. It is getting late and they have to get up for school tomorrow morning. They said they would be back early.
- Did they say anything about school?
- You know how hard it is to get any kind of news out of them. Can you imagine, my dear, how quickly passes the time? They will be graduating next year.
- True, so true.
- I try not to even think about it. I know when they start getting married my heart will feel it.
- Do not dramatize. It's going to be all right. There is still so much they have to learn.
- What do you think Mark will take up?
- I'm not sure but zoo technology seems quite possible.
- What about Andrzej?

- Well, that is a really tough
  one. Sometimes I think
  maybe he shouldn't be
  pressured so much with going
  to college.
- But he can't do physical labor.
- He can go to some post-high
  school program.
- Here they are!
- Good evening.
- Dad, this is my friend Ilona.
- Nice to meet you. Where is
  Basia?
- What Basia?
- Oh, come on – "what Basia".
  If you don't remember how
  can I?
- Oh, my! What happened to
  your head?
- Nothing, I hit myself on the
  tram.
- Don't believe him – Ilona
  started – He got into a fight at
  the party.
- Well, they got you good –
  father added.
- Dad, this is nothing. You
  should see the other guy.
- Sit down and tell me how was
  it?

Time was passing by and the boys were
talking and joking. Ilona tried to correct
them sometimes but only caused them to act
funnier. The parents really loved those
gatherings. In front of them were their two

33

sons and they could see how protective was one for another. Typical family get-together.

Andrzej was sitting on the couch listening to the music.

- "ABBA" – he thought – gorgeous women, great harmony of tunes, what a relaxing time.

He was glad to be alone now. It wasn't too often that he had the entire house just for himself.

- Do they all really like me? – he asked himself. – What do I give them that they want my company so much? I think the girls know I don't take them seriously. But what if they actually hope that I have some feelings for them. Well, it is a feeling of some kind, but what kind? I can't say I love them because this is not love. I don't love them even when I sleep with them and yet I have something for them that I can't describe. My life would have been so empty without them even if I love none of them. They are a part of my life and this is the part that I like so much. But – am I using them? What if they are using me? God, what am I thinking about here? What got in to me? – he thought.

34

Sound of the doorbell brought him back to reality as he went to open the door.

- Hi Danka.
- How are you? May I come in?
- Sure thing. I apologize but I kind couldn't stop looking at you. You look great. I haven't seen you like this before. Always the pants and now – look at you! What a dress, and the make up!

Danka got slightly embarrassed. He thought: "Again I keep talking and she's waiting". They both sat down. For the first time Andrzej started to feel uneasy. He simply didn't know what to talk about. Never before has he felt like that. Danka got came with the rescue. She came up to him and started kissing. The undressed in silence and made love for long time. Afterwards Andrzej took his guitar and started to sing: "I know you eyes like nobody else. They wouldn't lie to me. I stare at them once and I know it all. That day, the very first one, I knew they were awaiting the first night. You don't even know how much I awaited it".

Danka stared at him while putting on her clothes. When he finished singing she came up and gave him a kiss saying: "I took my chance, as you call it. Now I'm going home and please don't ask me if I want to see you again. We'll be friends like before."

She left. Andrzej continued sitting I surprise. He picked up his guitar again and continued on: "Perhaps with the others you will have more luck. Maybe somebody else will make you happy, Danka, but please remember this evening and the one who loved you".

He felt strange but somewhat pleased. Here TRAFILA KOSA NA KAMIEN.

Mark walked down the street while a black BMW pulled up and through the open window he heard someone's voice:

-   Mark! Six!
-   Seven! – he replied.
-   *Oki, doki, stop kidding. You ready for a ride?*
-   Sure.

The guy inside the car was a student of ATR. He was originally from Iraq. His Polish was good but he had this funny accent, which was the reason why Mark always teased him about the twisted pronunciation. Mark sat behind the steering wheel and they took off.

-   Wow, nice! I'll never afford it.
-   You know what? I have some U.S. dollars to sell. Interested?
-   Not myself but I'll ask my father if he wants some.
-   Do you want some jewelry, perhaps? Silver.
-   No. Andrzej is leaving for Germany so you may want to ask him. I'm pretty sure he would take some. Sweet car. Runs like the wind.
-   Doesn't it? Dad got it for me. Where do we want to go?

- Let's go to the "Medyk's".
- Sounds good.

Throughout this entire trip Mark was trying to figure out how to come across some money so that he could get a car like this. Certainly postgraduate college degree wasn't going to do it. "Maybe Andrzej is right not carrying about school and stuff at all. Maybe getting out on the market is an idea or some small business? Maybe…" – he thought. Various thoughts were running through his head with the speed of light. He wasn't able to focus. They reached their destination. Finally he could catch a breath. Both of them entered the club.

"Green horses kept on running and their KOPYTA shot with the DRZAZGI. Frogs in the pond toned the fire down and so the Moon lit up the stars. By the shore of the lake, you stood and looked listening to the voices of CZAJKI, surrounded by the summer scent of the greens TATARAK you said: how beautiful the summer with its mint scent, with its color of raspberries, the one of green forests, and of CZAJKI and KUKULKI".

- That was beautiful, Mark. Where did you hear that? - Pawel asked.
- Honestly, I don't remember. Somewhere while vacationing.
- Was it a poem or a song?
- A song but what difference does it make?

- We could use it at the end of the school year and sing before taking off for summer.
- Here at "Medyk's"?
- No, I was thinking at school.
- That's an idea. Pawel you are in charge of the program. If you want to I can sing it.
- You know what else do I need, Mark?
- What s it?
- Good and evil. Black evil and white good – symbolic gestures, a fight and at the end the good wins.
- I'll think of something.
- Thanks. Will you stay a little longer?
- No, I have to go.

He walked out on the street. Fresh air put him in excellent mood and he decided go walk for a while. He liked his town and walking it alone. Passing through the old market place and the Dluga St., stop by the big plaza where people always trade, buy and sell, - he loved it, and then catch the tram and head for home. From the opposite side of the street he heard the familiar voice.

- Mark! Mark!

He "woke up" and looked out. On the opposite side of the street there was a girl standing. We sometimes identify the places, the time or even the weather with how certain people looked in a particular moment. Girls sometimes dream about sensitive, peaceful boy who doesn't really stand out from the crowd but is short and slender reading the poetry. But sometimes they dream about this tall, well-built troublemaker fascinated with cars. And so do the boys – besides the quiet and balanced girls, dream about getting to know the crazy, sexy girls with wild personality.

Mark had the feeling that the girl he was about to meet is a sign of something that he still could not describe; yet her looks, the time of day and the season were in perfect harmony. "Someone is watching over me". – he thought.

- Hi, Aneta! - he shouted – After all those years!
- Oh, come on. It hasn't been that long.
- What are you doing in Bydgoszcz?
- I came to see my sister. I'll stay for a while.
- That's great, we can see each other more often.
- Definitely. What's been going on with you? Do you still play?
- Oh yes, just not as much as I used to. I want to finally graduate.
- Same here. Once I'm out of high school I want to move here and get in to WSP.
- That would be great. What are you doing for the summer?
- I don't really have any plans yet.

- Maybe we could go
  somewhere together.
- That sounds good.
- Ooops, here is my tram.
  We'll see each other soon,
  OK?
- Bye!

Once on the tram he started to think: "What got into me to offer taking her for vacation with me? Once Mirka finds out I'm dead. I like Mirka but she just doesn't stir me with life. Quite the opposite; she started to bore me. Crap! I'm starting to think like Andrzej. Well, maybe it's better this way".

When he arrived home he sat down at the table and started to scribble a letter to Mirka. "Do I love you still? Answer me. I guess somebody shut the door between us. You are still far away and I know that. And I don't want to mend it so that it gets better. Maybe this surprises you but oh, well. Perhaps it upset you – it is too late. I've waited for so long for some sign, some care. Our world filled with hurt, filled with tears still isn't so bad. The world knows that people won't change. Perhaps no – who really knows? Good-bye, Mirka! Mark".

As much as it was hard for him he also felt much better. "I will try with Aneta. We'll see what happens".

Memories of summer carry special character within themselves. We come back to some of them after many years and relive them with a doze of melancholy; the crowded buses and trains, the hitchhiking adventures, large forests from the shores of the Baltic Sea all the way to Mazury lakes and those never ending crop fields of Wielkopolska region. We see again the Karpatia area and the peaks of Tatry where crowds of people headed to hungry for strong emotions. People we met became life long friends and sometimes random summer flirtations led to weddings in the future. It is fascinating that so often the more we differ the closer we get to each other. There are so many countries that are well to do at first glance that suffer from this lack of unity. The geographic, language and religious barriers destroy the work of the people and sometime even transform into dangerous conflicts. Let's be proud that being from the north we spend those summer days in the south, or from the west we travel all the way to the east. This way or the other we always feel like we're at home. Boys we your guitars and girls with gorgeous hair – let's keep those camping fields and cabins a part of our beautiful scenario and keep on coming back.

Mark walked along with Andrzej. The girls were behind them.

- So how do you figure, Andrzej? – Who is going to pick all four of us up?

Mark wondered.

- Don't panic. If no one can pick all four of us we'll split.
- There is a semi. Ilona, start waving!

The truck stopped.

- Where do you guys want to go? – the driver asked.
- Koszalin! – everyone replied.
- I can only take two people.
- OK, Mark will go with Aneta. Ilona and I will get there later. Let's meet in Mielno on the bus station.

The car took off. Andrzej embraced Ilona and the two of them started to continue walking along the road trying to stop some car occasionally.

- Andrzej, I kind of don't like this whole hitchhiking idea.
- Why not? It'll save us some money and at the same time you can see some places.
- Yes, but all this is so uncertain and just really makes me tired.
- Do you know how many stories you can tell your friends after all this?
- I see you don't really care about how I feel and just focus on your goal regardless how you achieve it.
- You might be right but isn't it how the life kind of works
- Definitely not. You have to take opinions of others into consideration.
- Well, what if I dare to differ?
- There is always compromise, an alternative solution that would make everybody happy.

- Really? So what is your idea of compromise in our current situation?
- We can go back to town, get the tickets and get there on the bus.
- Wow, that really is something. I would never come up with anything alike. Well, if you want you can go back. I'm taking a hike.
- Fine. I'm coming back. You can keep on waiting for your luck.
- Well, then go! – Andrzej got mad all of the sudden and the two parted.

He arrived to Mielno but not after seven hours. "Not so bad" – he thought. Mark and Aneta were already waiting.

- What took you so long?
- Long? I don't think it was out of ordinary.
- Where is Ilona?
- She didn't like the idea and decided to go back.
- But she is coming on the bus, isn't she?
- I don't know and I don't care. Let's better go and see the sunrise.

The left.

- Isn't it beautiful?
- I love it. The sun looks so, sweet almost innocent. Whenever I look at the sunrise

43

I'm thinking about writing a
poem, and each time it would
be a different one. I guess it
depends on the mood.
Whenever you're sad the sun
helps you keeping to be sad
and vice versa – when you're
happy it laughs and dances
right with you. Maybe this is
its secret that it helps people
to feel whatever they want to
feel like?

- Listen guys, I have a bad news
– Andrzej said – All the
camping fields are filled up.
There might be a few spots
opening tomorrow.
- What are we going to do now?
– Aneta panicked.
- We'll sleep in the dunes! –
replied Andrzej
enthusiastically.

They went a little further away from the city
and found a quiet place in the dunes. At first
they chatted loudly Andrzej was somewhat
yielded at for this quite original sleeping
arrangement but once the sky lit up with the
gorgeous star scenario they gave up
complaining. Everyone was at awe looking
up to the sky. After a while Andrzej said:

- You know what, guys – it is
something else that you can
look at the sky for hours and
even though nothing really
changes there it keeps your
attention at its peak.

44

- It's not the sky itself that keeps your attention rather than you see there what you want to see. It is almost as if you were shooting your own film with camera of your imagination. The movie is so fascinating to you that you just don't want to stop watching. – Mark answered.
- You might be right, honestly, we always like to look at things that we want o see.

- Wake up! We're moving to the camping area.
- Is it you Andrzej?
- Hurry up before someone takes our spot!

When they had their tent set up they started to get to know their neighbors.
- Ania and Gosia from Krakow, and Jozek and Marcin from Katowice – Andrzej introduced.
- Good to meet you. – Mark and Aneta replied.

Days were passing by fast. By the sea they played and swam on ZAGLOWKA on the lake. Evenings brought many opportunities to dancing or playing the guitar by the fireplace. After a few days more friends from Bydgoszcz arrived and the fresh dose of cash allowed them to stay longer than originally planned.

- Andrzej, we're out of money.
  Time to go back.
- What are talking about, Mark.
  Just when I got to know Ania
  and Gosia you want me to just
  cut it short?
- How do you want to survive?
- With love! – Andrzej shouted.

The next day Andrzej went to the
neighboring village, Sarbinowo, and walked
into the "Baltic" restaurant.

- Hi, Darek.
- Little Andrzej! You've finally
  come.
- Yes, but I'm staying in
  Mielno.
- Well, stay at my place. You'll
  feel like at home.
- I know, but I have my brother
  and his girlfriend with me. I
  need some amber.
- Aaaa, the cash is gone?
- Yup.
- OK, I'll give you what I have
  and just pay me when you sell.
- Thanks a lot. You've just
  saved me one more week of
  vacation.
- No problem, anything for you.

They've known each other for years. Darek
lived in Sarbinowo to help his father on the
farm. In the summer time they were renting
a place to tourists. This is how he met
Andrzej and every year they spent at least
part of the summer together. Darek knew the
fishermen who would pick p some amber and

sell it to him a lot cheaper. Later on he would sell it to tourists for profit. When Andrzej sold he amber he bragged about the money he made in the tent. Everyone understandably applauded his resourcefulness. Along with a few guys they left to do some shopping. When they come back among the goods bought was a 100 liter large barrel of beer.

- Roll it out and start pouring!!! – Andrzej was screaming to Mark – Bring your guitar too!

A lot of people joined them with time. They set the fireplace up and time was passing by on drinking beer and singing. Mark was right next to Aneta and scribbled something on a piece of paper. After a few beer mugs he started to feel buzzed.

- I wrote a song. Give me a guitar!

Everybody got quiet. They listened as Mark's voice and the sound of music started to feel the forest.

"In a small town, among the bushes of BZY and KONWALIE there was a story told among old people that he listened to. It was the one about the sweet princess, asleep by a spell. It was the story about the knight that was to wake her up. Just like in a story – there is some truth in life. I wanted to find her – the sleeping beauty and walk her into new life. To love her with love unknown to the world… I no longer live in that small

47

town. I don't believe in fairytales or in magic either. I do, however, have my princess. Her knight is I – that's what I've become".

Once he finished everybody started to clap with enthusiasm.

- It's for you, Aneta. – he said.

They left after another week. Those were their last careless summer days of vacation. They returned tanned and filled with memories, which would last for years.

They surprise us once they arrive – the first months, which provide us with opportunities to test our own selves. We learn how to be patient and met the obligations. We also learn how to give as opposed to taking. We think with fear about the future and quite often so. What will it bring? Will we guide them so that they can become according to our wish? Or maybe the opposite – they will be far from our expectations. For years we ask questions and come to conclusion that our role in their life is just indirect. We pass along a lot of information hoping they would stay in their mind. We draw lines between good and evil, love and hate. For the most part we do a good job as teachers and parents. The greatest difficulty is when after years of hard work it comes to make a decision and we feel powerless to make it on our own. Whether we like it or not we have to give space and let our children decide for themselves. Graduation is the beginning. We all know the stress that the young people experience approaching their final high

school exams. It's their first serious test.
Whole families; brothers, sisters, aunts and
uncles, friends and teachers themselves await
the results impatiently. Sometimes one may
be under impression that it is everybody
around goes through this time with heavier
hearts than the students themselves. In a
way it only shows how important their future
is to them.

Mark sat in front of the school's entrance and
started to read a newspaper.
- Have you lost your mind? The tests begin
in 10 minutes and you're reading a paper? -
Krzysio could not believe his own eyes.

- What you want me to do;
study for 10 more minutes and
gather it all that I was
supposed to have learnt for the
past four years?
- Well no, but you could refresh
something a little bit.
- Sorry, Krzychu but I don't
think so. I believe relaxing
before the exams will do you
more good than reading stuff
you wouldn't even understand
'cause you're so stressed out.
Andrzej was standing nearby talking to
Alina.
- You know, one day I didn't
feel like going to school so
Grzegorz and I went fishing.
We took all the stuff, bucket
and nets ad here we were,
marching through the old

49

market place to catch a tram. All of the sudden the chemistry teacher's voice above us went: "And where the two of you think you're going?" Stupid me, taken by surprise replied: "To a dentist". She just looked at us, then at our WEDKI and nodded. The next day both of us had a lot of explanation to do at the principal's office.

Both Andrzej and Alina laughed at his story. She said:

- Andrzej, there is two minutes left – aren't you nervous at all?
- Polish is a piece of cake. It's the math that may not go so smooth.

They walked in to the auditorium. The final test known as "Matura" was about to begin. Like it was expected the Polish language test went with no major stressing out or drama. The day math exam was to take place was, however, marked by significant nervousness and fear. Many college students came to help out the prospective future college students. In front of the school groups of people were studying and making up for the forgotten or never learnt facts in an impressive pace. All around one could here repetition of various rules and formulas. To those who have never had an experience of the *matura* exam climate it might have seemed like the young people were so hungry for knowledge that didn't even want to waste a pause between classes. It was quite the view and in a good way. The care and willingness to help the younger ones by those already in college was a sign of a particular connection that existed and was being passed on between youths from different generations. Isn't it what us – the "older ones" wanted?

Andrzej finished reading the results and took a deep breath. His smile went from one ear all the way to the other one. He said:
- It's over. That's it!

The Graduate's Ball was the peak of our high school life's history. Some of those young people would never see each other again. Others – quite the opposite – will remain friends.
Mark was walking proudly with his head up to the rhythm of traditional "Polonaise".
- I wonder when will be the next time I'll dance Polonaise"? – he whispered to his partner.
- I'm sure there will be more than one occasion.
- I don't know about it. Wherever I go there is this trendy contemporary beat going on. Like the music – like the dancers. There is less and less of the traditional balls with elegant women and men in tuxedos.
- Times change, Mark.

- They may be changing but soon it will be up to us to shape the reality.
- So it worries you so much that you're the only one left who enjoys "Polonaise"?
- Yes, that's exactly how I feel.
- Well, you're wrong. Look, everybody's dancing smiling and you can see they enjoy it just as much.
- It's just the cover up. If you gave them a chance they would quickly change this evening into a disco party.
- And you can't forbid them that, Mark. You're neither the king nor the president to dictate the people what to do. And if you ever become one in the future, you have to earn their confirmation.
- I already have such.
- From who?
- From the king who gave my great great grandfather the nobility title. It passes from father onto the son.
- You're kidding, right?

No answer.

- If you're serious, remember one thing: not everything that's good for you is equally good for others.

The music finished. Mark took his partner's hand and kissed it.

52

-   Thank you, Madame, for this
    precious and noble advise. –
    he said.

Hey walked away to the table.

-   Just because you've graduated
    from high school doesn't
    mean you can drink like a fish
    – said Andrzej.
-   What can I do about the fact
    that here they give you beer,
    somewhere else wine and yet
    somewhere else the vodka?
-   And you have to be like a
    tanker and take everything
    that someone's pouring in
    you? What is that girlfriend
    of yours gong to think? Oops,
    I forgot her name was
    "Zytnia". Now you have a
    new one and her name is
    "Toilet Bowl".
-   Andrzej, stop torturing me. –
    Rysio said it lifting his head
    up off the toilet bowl.
-   I don't mean to put you down
    but I don't want to sit here all
    evening and look at you
    puking.

Andrzej left and walked towards the
ballroom when Basia approached him.

-   I'm leaving, Andrzej, just
    wanted to say bye.
-   You're leaving already?
-   Yes, I'm leaving for Krakow
    in just two days.

53

- You will be back though, right?
- No, that's the point. I will be staying at my aunt's and try to get to acting school.
- Now you're telling me this?
- Andrzej, I had tried but you just were always too busy. I know you're with new girlfriend now, Ilona, but that's beyond the point. I just wanted you to know that I cared for you and there was something there for you that I felt. It's the past now. I just wanted to wish you everything best in the future, that's all.

Andrzej just stood there not knowing what to say or do. In a fraction of the second the whole time they knew each other just flashed through. Times when he carried her in the sea and when he taught her jumping to water at the lake, their passionate love they were making while in the tent and times he shared with her his artistic plans. They've known each other for so many years, yet he never thought she actually might care. She was the first girl that wished him luck upon parting. He embraced her and said:
- Basia, thank you for everything. Please don't think of me bad.

He watched her walking away and waited – maybe she will turn back and wave good-bye. She didn't.

He returned to the bathroom and grabbed
Rysiek by his hand.

- We're getting the hell out of
  here.
- Why? Andrzej, I'm already
  feeling better.
- Maybe you are but I'm not. I
  feel like having a cocktail.
  Keep me company?
- Sure.

The left the ball and took off to a restaurant.

This is how our feelings or friendships
sometimes reach their end. They exist as
long as we keep them alive. Sometimes we
don't realize that we are an important part of
somebody else's life. Sometimes others
don't understand how much they mean to us.
Is this the result of luck of communication o
is it our personally boast that prevents us
from admitting. It would be so much easier
to live had we known what to expect from
others.

Andrzej was in taxicab thinking – "life would
be so boring if we knew everything about
everybody right away".

College entrance exams were even more
stressful than high school finals. It was nice
to hear, however, about our friends being
accepted. What used to be our dreams now
was about to become reality.
Time flies - the saying goes. We sometimes
brush it off but only until its message starts
knocking on our own door. Thousands of

young people begin to shape their own paths of lives taking it seriously and responsibly. But as the time goes by they give in to the student life reality. Tests, quizzes and exams – they all contribute to the fact that all of the sudden… this is the sophomore year around the corner already. Tight schedule intertwined with heavily drunk parties makes us realize quickly that studying is an art of survival. Students' hangout places do not need advertising. They're always filled up to the capacity and very self-reliant. One can often run into students who aren't students just for the sake of gaining a degree or the knowledge itself. They just love the student's life, the academia. Their goal is to be a student. Fashionable beards and mustache along with first signs of deficit of hair are there to confirm that we're dealing here with a "perpetual student". All colleges in our country are great; some rich in their own history while others less marked by tradition but one thing is certain: they're all there to serve us all and do so brilliantly. Mark was running around the house frantically looking for some shirt that would be appropriate. He had a date with Aneta and wanted very much to look good. He usually dressed well anyway faithfully believing that you never know whom you'll meet and in what circumstances. "They see you the way you look" – his father used to say. This is one of the rules he always remembered. When he got to the place Aneta was already there.

- Hi, Aneta. You look great!

- Thank you, you look handsome yourself.
- Here is a flower for you. – he said and gave her a rose.
- Just with no particular reason?
- Every time I see you is the perfect reason.
- Very nice of you.
- Remember, it wasn't that long ago when we were dreaming about getting to college. I'm a sophomore already and don't even feel it yet. Time really flies.
- I feel the same way.
- All I do is sit over the books all day long. I sometimes think maybe the zoo technology was not such a great idea.
- You can always change majors.
- I'm not going to mix things up now. If I started this I might as well finish. So good that we can pop to a club or so from time to time.
- You like to dance and don't even try telling me that you're only going to clubs for me, because I like it. You are excellent and like dancing just as much as I do. – Aneta said.
- Fine, fine, you're right.

They finally arrived to the club. Once they entered right away a group of friends surrounded them. Almost everybody knew each other. Strong music and effective lights boosted everybody's energy level. Walking through tables one could hear some couples whispering to each other, then political debates or great artistic debuts. Sober or drunk, everyone wanted to give proof to the world that they're worthy of the great title of being a college student. After the party Mark took Aneta to the dormitory.

- It's very late. I really don't feel like going home. – he said.
- You can sleep at my place.
- How will I get in? They won't let me to girls' dormitory.
- Right, I forgot.

He kissed her gently and started to walk towards the street. Aneta walked into her place. As he was walking himself, he thought: "Why is it that I have to go home when I simply don't want to? I want to be with her today, now. Why do I always have to follow some rules and orders? What would be so wrong about spending a night with girl? Overall I am an adult now."
He stopped.
"That's it". He didn't go back home but returned to the dormitory. He attempted to get in through the back rather then front entrance.
"I'll get in trough the window". – he thought – "...but how? It's on the tenth floor!"
He grabbed on to lightning rod and started to climb. On the second floor he knocked at the

window but nobody answered. He kept on climbing; third floor – no answer, fourth - the same thing. Once he reached the fifth he looked down.

"Damn! It's high. If I lose it I'm done" – he thought. He knocked at the window and all of the sudden a light went off. "Thanks God" – he thought. The window opened and the girl inside said:

- What are you doing? Are you crazy?
- Let me in, I'm about to lose it.
- I can't.
- Listen, I'm not a thief. I just want to get to see my girlfriend.
- Get in and get out!
- Thanks a lot. You've really saved my life.

Initially he thought it was a good joke but then he realized that in fact that was true. He started to walk down the hallway. He decided not to use the elevator and just run up the stairs. He reached Aneta's room and knocked.

- Oh my, how did you get here?
- Quite simply, I walked up the stairs.
- Whatever, they wouldn't let you in. Get in before someone sees you. Tll me how did you get here?
- Through the window.
- On the first floor?
- No on the fifth.

-   Dear God, you could have
    died!
-   It was close.
-   I didn't expect something like
    this from you.

She looked at his hands.

-   You've cut yourself.

He looked at them and saw that indeed his
hands were cut along way. Blood was mixed
with dirt and pieces of concrete.

-   Come on; let's take care of
    you.

When she finished washing his cuts they sat
down on the bed. The darkness quickly
surrounded their first night together.

Four TREFLE, pass, Royal Flush!

-   What are you saying?
-   Have you ever played
    BRYDZ?
-   What are you talking about?
-   I'm trying to get the Aces, you
    moron.
-   Oh, I see!
-   All right, that's enough of
    exchange of information – the
    third voice added.
-   Are we playing or what?
-   I'm sorry but I've had enough.
    We've been playing since the
    early afternoon – Andrzej
    said.
-   What you suggest we do?
-   Get some beer and some girls.
-   I like it.

- Zbyszek will get the beer and we'll meet back again at 10. Everyone brings their own beauty.
- Sounds like a plan.

When Andrzej was at the stop he spotted a girl.

- Hi, where are you heading to, if I may ask – he started the conversation.
- To the Old Town, going to "Medyk's".
- I heard it was a cool place with cool people but I've never been there yet – he kept lying.
- Really? That's impossible.
- Seriously, I have to tell you something but promise it will stay between us.
- OK, what's the secret?
- See, everyone thinks I'm such a looser and the guy very much on the shy side. Maybe they're right. I am shy.
- But you started talking to me at the stop.
- I started talking to you because see, a few friends of mine and I played cards and they kept on laughing at me that I still don't have a girlfriend etc. They bet me that I won't fin one either until 10 p.m. tonight. I didn't know what to do and fate wanted me

to meet you. So this is why I
started talking to you – I don't
want to be laughed at my
whole life.
The girl looked at him with expression of
understanding on her face.

- I don't know, maybe it's
  inappropriate of me to ask you
  for a favor that you go with
  me so that I can show my
  friends that I can have my
  own girl – he was lying to the
  extremes of decency.
- No big deal, I will go with you
  but I can't stay for long – she
  answered with a smile.
- Sure thing and I thank you
  very much! What is your
  name?
- Marlena, what's yours?
- Andrzej.

When Mark woke up he looked around the
room. The little, familiar place felt especially
cozy now. Aneta was still asleep. He
dressed and left quickly. It was still early
and so when he walked out the lady in charge
asked:

- How did you get here, mister?
- I just popped in a second ago
  but I didn't see anybody yet.
  I'm leaving right now.

The lady at the window just waved her hand
with disbelief.
"It's a lot easier to get out than to get in" – he
thought.

He felt happy. Aneta was never too demanding. She respected his opinion and liked making love to him. All put together put him in great mood.

"If this is what marriage is like I can get married even today" – he thought.

Andrzej was making scrambled eggs at the same time peeking into the room where Marlena was laying.

- Would you like some?
- No thank you. God, it's morning already? I don't even know when I fell asleep.

"She didn't know" – he thought – "but she sure knew all the positions. She really wore me out".

They were at Andrzej's friend's place; the same where they played cards just a day before. Party was a flop because they all came empty handed. Andrzej was the only one to bring a girl, Aneta. They had some beer and played the guitar. The two of them ended up in bed. Now as he was eating breakfast all he wanted was to get rid of the girl ASAP.

- You know what, Andrzej?
- What?
- You really aren't all that shy like you said you were. They way you talked to me later on – I knew you had tricked me. I'm willing to forgive you if you take me to the movies.

"Movies" – he thought – "How about the wedding chapel". He lost appetite.

- Marlena, get up. My mother
  is in the hospital and I
  promised I would go and see
  her at 10.
- You didn't mention anything
  about your mom being in the
  hospital.

"Because she's not, you stupid" – he thought.

- I didn't mean to worry you or
  anything.

When they left Andrzej called the cab and
out her in it.

- I'll call you today – he said.
- Please, I'll be waiting.

The taxi took off. Andrzej felt relieved.
"That was kind of dangerous" – he thought as
he was leaving for home. Mark was waiting
for him at the door.

- You better don't talk to mom.
- What happened? It's probably
  the night away problem isn't
  it? I'll take care of that.
- You not coming home for the
  night is one thing. I didn't
  come either.

For a moment Andrzej stood there evidently
surprised.

- Congrats, bro! You finally
  start to act like a real student.
  Who was the lucky girl?
- How do you know it was a
  girl?
- Don't tell me you're a homo
  and sleep with boys.

- No, no – Mark answered embarrassed – I was at Aneta's.
- Perfect choice, my brother. She is worthy to sin with.

They talked for a very long time covering areas of love affairs and various incidents with friends, card game nights... Andrzej was listening to Mark who always was well spoken, putting sentences in organized manner. He also always could logically back his argument. Mark on the other hand enjoyed the chaotic reports coming from Andrzej, mixed with good humor and very spicy, vulgar dictionary. At the end they both summoned up their academic success stories. Mark was a student of zoo technology and Andrzej attended post high school courses in radio and TV production. They were so very different yet so close and alike. One thing was certain: they completed each other perfectly. It is conversations such as theirs that sometimes remind us how much we need each other.

What does future hold for us, and what other adventures are ahead of us? How many happy days and how many sad ones? The good ones are always too short while the ones filled with trouble drag. This is when we wish we could turn back time so that we could use it up in a different way. We are who we are and the younger years are the ones that help us find our own identities. Let us rejoice therefore that in the early years of our lives we have to carry pens and notebook rather than guns or handcuffs. It is our responsibility to make sure that future generations pass the same traditions onto the next ones. Let's laugh and joke about those younger years and be happy that they helped us so much in becoming the way we are.

Chapter II

Without any particular expression Mark and Andrzej were listening to the sound of soil falling on the oak coffin. Leon Polskowicz has passed away. He left at the age that was suitable for rest and enjoyment of everything he had worked for so hard. Hundreds of people came to pay the last tribute to their boss, neighbor, and friend. He was 44. Sudden death brings about so much disappointment, anger and disbelief. Many give up once faced with its reality. So often people say that life is one big question mark, that God is unfair and that planning the future is pure stupidity. Everyone is entitled to their own beliefs. But let's think for a moment: what would life be if it weren't for our desires, dreams as well as problems and aspirations? Can we really say that short life is the wasted life? How to think about the young boys giving up their lives in wars or uprisings assuring our own freedom today? Each life has its purpose and meaning. In the times of peace the purpose of every man's life is the well being of his family.

Who was Leon Polskowicz? Born in Vilna he couldn't really enjoy much time studying or playing because of the turmoil of war. Au contraire: those were 70 years of struggle to survive. Armies of Germany or Russia have only signified bad news. After the war, when the Russians took away eastern part of Poland, the Polskowicz family moved to the heart of the country. Leon graduated from college and worked in paper factory. He was climbing up the latter of hierarchy quickly ultimately becoming the CEO. His professional career, however, was not his biggest accomplishment. Being a father was that made his life fulfilled and happy. That's right – the fatherhood.

At first glance it seems like such an easy task. Looking deeper into it one can notice that it's far more complicated. Every father can recall his first adventures with the diapers. Then the long walks with the stroller until the light of our life begins to walk on its own. If you're a father of a boy the most important moment, however, is just about to come. The magical and unforgettable time comes when you introduce the boy to the word "soccer ball".

So many wonderful and joyful moments we spend in the company of our beloved kids. We explain the rules of the game, tricky passes and strategic maneuvers. Soccer and handball, volleyball and basketball, water polo and ping-pong make the time pass quickly and happily till the moment comes when they start to spend more and more time with their peers. The question: "Dad, can we go and play?" starts to be asked less and less frequently. We start to take position on the side.

Pride and satisfaction reappears when we watch our kids perform in school tournaments and contests. We think: "He is so good at that. This is my work at works…" Interestingly enough it is not until very late in life that the fathers finally receive proper thanks and gratitude for their work. How many times we see on TV big sport events after which the winners give interviews. When asked for a few words the sportsman usually says: "I'd like to say hallo to my mom". But this is part of father's reality and we hardly ever complain. Truthfully there are not too many people to whom to come and whine. We simply go back to our duties, our jobs and our homes. We have to stay strong in order to assure the family's well being and be ready to address the most complicated issues. Dreams of fathers wait patiently the moment when grown up children will share stories of their successes and start providing for their parents. But those dreams often don't come true. Every day reality proves that the older the children the more care they need.

Mark was standing by the graveside. "…And his name shall be Forty and Four" – he recalled asking himself what this prophecy of Mickiewicz had to do with his father? "Is it just a coincidence of numbers? How will all this go on? He always knew what to do in every situation. Will I do OK in life?" – he wondered.

- I am so sorry, Mark. - Aneta said.
- Thank you.
- I really liked your dad. His death is a terrible shock to me.
- I know, I just don't know what to do, Aneta. Should I continue going to school or

take up some job? We have to survive somehow. Andrzej won't hold on to a job. Mom need care, so does the house. I don't even know where to begin? "Solidarity" grows in strength. What if the Soviets invade?

- Stop talking nonsense – Andrzej interrupted their conversation – I have just buried you father and first thing you do is panic right away. Remember when we played soccer with dad in the forest, or how we sat by the stream? What was he used to saying? "Whatever life brings, boys – remember – you are the Polskowicz and it means there are no obstacles you wouldn't be able to overcome. All you need is your will. History of our family goes back to 5th century. We've been through a lot already and never in a situation from which nowhere to go".

- I do remember that very well – Mark answered.

- So get yourself together and stop dramatizing. We'll trade stuff and make money. We'll go to Germany, to Czech and Hungary and it will work out

somehow. We'll graduate
from college – not much left
to finish. Mom does work
still. Everything should stay
as it was. The Soviets won't
invade because this would
mean a huge uproar in the
entire Europe. At the end
"Solidarity" will reach a deal
with the government and it
will be all right. Just don't
think too much, please.

Mark was listening in silence and his mood
somewhat got better.

- You're right, bro. We'll do as
you say and see where things
will go.

If their father were alive he would have been
proud. They lost the strongest pillar of their
lives but have proven to be mature enough to
make some tough decisions. It looked like
they were ready, indeed, to face the problems
that were to come in the future.

Short life proved not to be the wasted one.
Polskowicz has not left. He stayed in mind
and hearts of the two young men. This is
why fathers don't dwell on thinking about
death. They live their lives day by day
without waiting for songs of praise and glory.
One thing we ought to promise them is our
remembrance.

Looking through the window in sunny winter
day it feels like as if the Sun covered the
snow gently with its coat. Millions of
invisible rays kindly meet the white surface.

Taking a closer look we recognize particular paths through which icy crystals that shine at us with the silver gleaming. They travel sometimes in various directions however the wind will tell them to. Picking up a flake of snow we observe it fascinated. Its perfect structure puts us at awe. We don't know what to call the color of snow covered by he rays of sun. Every winter has its own character. Some are long while others only last for a while. They bring back memories of joyful winter break – these are the happy winters. If our girlfriend dumps us – these are the sad ones. Then there are the very cold winters or – almost to tease – the warm ones too.

The winter of 81' was bad. Cold, cloudy days were marked by heavy snow. Life had only black and white colors. Even cars painted in different colors were unable to mend the ever-present sense of darkness. Strikes, negotiations with the authorities, empty store shelves – those were the markings of every day life.
Poland became divided; on those who were pro-Walesa and those against him as well as those who simply did not care.

> - I just don't get it – Mark said – It's clear we have to abandon communism. When I listen to some people I just can't believe they are willing to negotiate with the communists.

73

- That's life – Grzegorz mumbled.
- What do you mean? Look around – there's nothing. Mustard and vinegar is all you have in stores. How do you imagine the future? You'll graduate and then what?
- It's simple; we'll start working, take the leading positions and – with time – the power as well. Eventually we'll have it our way.
- Nonsense. It takes decades and within the next few years the Soviets will bring so much military you won't be able to move around. We need reasonable system in this country. Look at black market – everything! If the government freed the market the situation would change very fast. People are being lied to constantly. They complain about the system, crack jokes about it yet now, when there's a chance to change the situation they do nothing.
- People keep quiet because they're afraid to loose whatever it is they have already.
- And what is it that they have? A TV set and a crappy 126p?

What's the use of having a car
if there may be no electricity,
or a car – even crappy – if
there's no gasoline?

- But everybody has a job and a
  place to live.
- Hey, Grzesiu, you talk like
  one of "them". So what if
  everyone's employed? When
  was the last time your
  government told you about
  "how much we've done" or
  how much we spent and for
  what, how much is left, huh?
  Wherever you looked –
  everything looked great;
  beautiful hospitals, farms,
  factories. How come none of
  that has ever gone bankrupt or
  had problems, whatsoever?
  And where are we now?
  You've got your "ratio
  square" to live off – that's all.
- Mark, do you seriously
  believe that capitalism will
  satisfy everyone's needs?
- Oh, Grzegorz – Mark sighed.
- It gives nothing for free and
  never will.
- But it does not control your
  life by telling what and how to
  do. Whatever decisions you
  make about your life – it's on
  you. Poverty and richness
  will always be neighbors.

Equality – now, that's dangerous.
- Give it up now, Mark – I can tell we have different views of the future. On the other hand I am glad we could have this conversation.
- Just because we differ on things is not a problem, Grzesiu. I just want to avoid a situation when you believe you possess absolute truth.
- And why is that?
- Because most likely I would then believe that it is all totally untrue.
- So?
- We would be on opposite sides. When we are on opposite sides we begin to say and do things just in order to prove that it is I who is correct. It leads to a situation when we forget what is it that we tried to argue. All we know is that we are against each other. This is how many friendships end and what's more scary – nations fail. It is something we should remember from our history.
- Hey, Mark, it's going to be all right – Grzegorz said – I am just trying to think a little bit like and put myself in shoes of people who are older, who

have experienced life and have no desire to ever again watch some disorder evolve.

- Just because they've been trough some stuff does not entitle them to take away our own right to experience whatever it is that's suitable for our age or the right to choose the way we want to live – Mark continued.

They were walking down the street and the conversation seemed not to have an end. They only differed at first glance. They simply had different outlooks on life. One thing, however, that united them, and righteously so, was hunger for change in their lives. Regardless on how much they differed from each other, they shared one common goal – their future.

Andrzej and Arek drove up to the supermarket.

- Arek, grab the bags and let's hurry. Are you sure they delivered? 100%? A friend called me up.

They popped into the store and looked around like professionals.

- All right – Andrzej said – I will see Mrs. Ela and ask if we can start packing.

Arek just stood there looking ahead of him – the entire supermarket was completely empty. Two clerks were walking back and forth along the wall. There were no

customers because there was nothing to buy.
Empty shelves were shining with their…
emptiness. Arek felt uncomfortable, all of
the sudden.

- Come here, quickly! –
  Andrzej yelled.

Arek "woke up" and marched towards
Andrzej who started to quickly give
instructions:

- We'll take five cases. We
  have to repack them – they
  don't want to give those
  plastic ones.
- I thank you very much, Mrs.
  Ela – Andrzej said to the store
  manager – You're the best.
  Here you go, a chocolate for
  you.
- Gee! So much beer! – Arek
  screamed – It'll last for a
  whole week.
- It just seems like that. It'll be
  gone in an hour.

They both started to laugh. Once they had all
the beer in the car they took off towards their
part of town. Andrzej was humming a song;
"I get up at 7; quick breakfast and by 8 I'm
by the store drinking my beer. At 9 am I'm
already wandering the streets – like a
scavenger animal wounded by a bullet. This
is when I look for a lady that would hold me
in the afternoon. And at night – I will be
tired yet feeling so young, as the young girl
in a little bed whispers to my ear: *you're so
beautiful*".

- Oh, would you please stop with those sleazy serenades? – Arek said.
- They're not sleazy at all rather than ballads about life.
- Fine, call it whatever. Why don't you come up with a ballad about no beer in the entire town? You have to have friends in the industry to get some.
- You don't need a ballad about it – everybody knows – Andrzej replied.
- They know now but in a few years they'll forget. People will think we're idiots when we just tell them that we *managed* to get five cases of beer. They'll think we're bragging.
- Don't you have any other worries? - Andrzej asked.
- Besides the fact that I have to bring this government down and create a brand new one, plus improve the situation of some 30 million people – no, I don't have any other worries.

They all laughed.

- You know what? – Andrzej began – We're joking now and that's all good but what if in fact nothing changes and there will be still nothing to buy; no food, no beer. Holidays are

79

coming – I really think
sometimes that it's some
punishment that we live in the
world we live.
- And I look at it differently,
Andrzej. It isn't punishment
but a favor. Whatever
happened had to happen and
now is time to change
everything once and for all.
- Speaking of food – do you
have anything at your place to
munch? – Andrzej asked.
- Nothing really.
- So how do you live, and with
your brother?
- We've finished everything last
night. Parents are coming
back Saturday so we'll survive
somehow.

Andrzej kept quiet. The first words coming
from Arek's brother mouth once they came
home were: "Do you guys have something to
eat?"

- Hmm, we have no bread and
no butter anymore, but maybe
you'd like some beer? – Arek
asked him.

The three of them stood there for a second
not knowing what to say or do. In the end
they all started to laugh.

- Come on, boys! Dinner's
ready!
- We'll be right there, mom.

Andrzej was finishing to scribble something in his notebook while Mark was looking through the records.

- What's the date today? – Andrzej asked.
- December 12th, why?
- Well, there will be a band playing during a party at "Lotnik". The guitar player is our teacher.
- Are you serious? I didn't know that Bielen started to play at parties. I can't believe this. He plays the classical stuff so nicely.
- Get Aneta ands let's go together at 8.
- Cool. Should we take the car?
- No, who's going to drive if we get drunk?
- OK, I'll cover the cab.
- And I'll get us on the bus.
- What are you boys now up to?
- Nothing mom, we'll just go dance a little.
- You're not taking the car, are you?
- No, if we drink why looking for trouble?
- I didn't; mean that but tomorrow is the 13th and the demon is wide-awake.

"Lotnik" was a military people's club right by the Bydgoszcz airport. Its greatest celebrity was Hermaszewski – the first Polish astronaut in space. The party was going excellent and indeed what Andrzej said about their teacher being in the band turned out to be true. After the end everyone remained in great mood.

- Oh my, it is cold. I hope we'll catch something home really quickly. I don't care; but or a cab, just fast, please.
- Don't whine, Mark, something will come around.
- It is the 13th already. I guess we really are out of luck. I haven't seen that few buses passing by ever, in fact I didn't see a single one. Strange.

- Get up right away! Mark, Andrzej – get up now! - Their mother's voice was loud.
- Where is the fire mom?
- There is war not the fire.

The boys got off their beds instantly.

- What are you talking about?

General Jaruzelski was addressing the nation. Purpose: to inform the nation that beginning December 13th, 1981 Martial Law was being introduced in Poland.

Andrzej was desperately trying to call up some friends. No chance – the phones are off. Mark rushed out from the house to see if there are any Soviet tanks yet. Mom was trying to get some more information on the radio but everything kept quiet.

It was a very cold winter that year. Snow and cloudy skies dressed the entire world in black and white. People, on the other hand, succumbed to the atmosphere, acting as if the country was in the grieving process.

The market place – so gently incorporated in the city's reality, serves almost as an arrow indicating the direction in which to go. It's like a dot over letter "i" – completes – and definitely is the center of every day life. Whether in winter or spring, this is the place for children to play. For its service to the people, they decorate it with nice KLOMB, a fountain, a monument or commemorative plaque. A narrow street leads us towards the church. Its arrow-like shape brings back the gothic times. In a shadow of its monumental structure there is a small wooden church from the Middle Ages, standing there almost as if forgotten. It is the St. Procop's church. Simply decorated with stone interior it takes us back to the beginning of Christianity. How many years have passed? How many people stood their foot in this church? How many prayers were said echoing through the stones? Mark was sitting on the pew and thought: "What was it that people would ask God a 1000 years ago? Did they have similar doubts to mine? I'm getting married tomorrow and still am uncertain whether this is the right decision. I don't want to disappoint anybody; my wife, my children and myself. Perhaps it's natural? Maybe everyone goes through the same dilemmas, which, with time, fade away. I will work and try to turn my dreams into reality. My wife will support me. This is what marriage is supposed to be about, isn't it?" – he thought at the same time hoping to hear some voice of confirmation. His thoughts, however, was all that he could hear.

- Bitters, bitters, bitters! – the guests were shouting according to old tradition while tapping their knives on the glasses.

Mark embraced Aneta and kissed her.

- Bravo! One more time, come on! – loud shouting did not stop.

Andrzej was dancing with his new girlfriend in the room next door.

- This is a very nice wedding – she said.
- Sure thing. It's my brother getting married. You have no idea what we had to go through in order to get the food and vodka. Times are as they are. Love does not wait. I have fiends who work in stores and restaurants so that's why we have plenty of everything. The worst problem was the place. In restaurants they told us "only till midnight". So, we decided to do it at home.
- I really admire your resourcefulness.

84

- Oh, stop. "Admire" – there
  are many other thins I know
  worthy of admiration.
- Like what?
- Come with me to the car and
  I'll show you.

- Karol, where is Andrzej? –
  Mark asked.
- What you mean? – in the
  usual place.
- That being?
- With a girl, alone, in some
  hidden spot. I can't believe
  you have to ask.
- I guess, if he didn't make love
  to all the girls in some corner
  it would mean something's
  wrong.

Krzysiek came up to Mark and said:
- Congrats, my friend,
  seriously.
- Thank you, my friend. It's
  just a shame not everyone
  showed up. Some of the
  people were probably a bit
  afraid; others didn't want to
  deal with the whole "obtain
  permit from the police" stuff.
  But the young crowd showed
  up.
- You have to understand – I
  mean this is MARTIAL LAW
  time.

- I hope there will be a day
  when we all will look at it in a
  different light.

OCZEPINY were the main point of the evening. Music, dancing, toasts – there was no end to any of it. Not a single person felt this wedding was taking place during the Martial Law Time. The tension was detectible when uncle Kaz was telling his stories of the Home Army, surrounded by the crowd of youths. Names like Monte Cassino, Battle of England, and The Warsaw Uprising were popping up quickly and sharp. Hearing risen voices, women tried to quiet down the male crowd. Grandmas and aunties were priceless in the amount of heart-felt advices they were giving to the bride. Guests were from al over the country; some completely strange to each other. There was something very precious about how this wedding day brought everyone together to the point where they discussed history and future alike. One more time the old saying that "all Poles are one large family" has proven to be true.

- Just look how much I make
  per month – that's ridiculous!
  For what was all that
  schooling and stuff? – Andrzej
  was visibly aggravated. – I
  don't need some almsgiving.
  There is no way I'm gonna
  make it there. Old employees
  are taking over all the
  assignments while I'm stuck

working on old speakers and
black n' white TV's. Screw
this crap! All I'm going to et
from this is long lasting
cramps.
- Chill out. We'll figure
  something out – Mark tried to
  calm him down.
- I already have an idea.
- What?
- I'll sell the 126p. We'll get
  the 125 p model and use as a
  cab.
- Who's going to be driving?
- I will – Andrzej answered
  quickly – and you better move
  on with this college stuff, as
  soon you'll be the daddy. You
  need to provide your family
  somehow. A cab would be
  helpful. I'll chip in as much
  as I can until you get on your
  own feet.
- - Mom, can you come up here
  for a minute?
- What's going on, boys?
- I would like to try to sell the
  car and get a larger one so that
  we can start driving a taxicab.
  What do you think about that?
  – Andrzej started.
- You know what, I was kind of
  waiting for you to come up
  with something like this. I see
  how you, Andrzej, struggle at
  work. I honestly though,

didn't think you would come
up with a taxicab idea. Do
you think you should think it
through a bit more?

- No, it has been thought
  through already – Andrzej
  answered.
- So, what do you think?
- Do what you think is best.
  You are adults.

Andrzej started working on everything
enthusiastically. Within a month he was able
to sell the little Fiat and buy the larger model.
He also got a meter and properly set it up.
Meanwhile he passed the necessary tests on
topography of town and road tests. He filled
out all the necessary paperwork and after
three months received the license e had
waited for so much. Mark was observing all
of this with a surprise. He's never before
seen him working so hard and so diligently.

- Open up the champagne! –
  Andrzej shouted.
- Where am I supposed to get
  it?
- I brought it myself.
- What happened – you getting
  married or what?
- No, I'm not that crazy. We got
  the license today! The
  numbers are: 1460. "14" is
  the day of my birth and 60 the
  year I was born. Is this great
  or what?

They sat for a long time talking about the plans they had with respect to the taxicab. They sipped on champagne and were just truly happy that finally they had something on their own that would bring them some money. Mom and Aneta were pleased too. Everyone hoped that this family situation soon would improve.

- Will you have one more? – a guy asked Andrzej.
- No, that's enough. I don't want to drive trashed.
- I like that – stranger replied – Listen, I'm looking for someone I can trust to deliver stuff all over the country.
- What kind of stuff? – Andrzej asked.
- Good vodka, whiskey and cigarettes, and chocolate.
- What's in there for me?
- I'll pay you like for the regular trip.
- Nope. I'll get more for the gas just driving around town.
- How much do you want?
- Triple. Plus you pay my room and board should I need it.

A man thought for a while and finally said:
- Double, plus the room and board.
- No, you need to find somebody else – Andrzej said and stood up from the table.

- Where do you think you're
  going? I'm not done yet.
Andrzej sat back, somewhat surprised. "That
would be something if he agreed". He
thought.
- Never in my life did I have to
  pay that much. But you've
  got a good rep so I'll take my
  chance. You'll get the triple
  plus room and board. Deal?
They shook hands to seal the deal. Andrzej
breathed deeply inside of him. "Double
would be good too, but this is just great", he
thought.
- We start tomorrow at 9 going
  to Gdansk.

- How is my dear wife feeling
  today? – Mark asked.
- How formal of you! – Aneta
  replied.
- I'm just asking like this – still
  can't get used to it. The little
  one is on its way and I still am
  getting used to the fact that I
  am married. Have you
  thought of the names?
- If it were a boy his name
  would be Roman. If it's a girl
  – Krystyna.
- I'm not sure about them –
  Mark said.
All over again - they were flipping through
the pages of the calendar thinking about
possible names. It took them a very long
time and sometimes their voices were getting

a little loud. Finally they had their pick: Ana and Jan.

- How is Andrzej and his taxi driving? – Aneta asked.
- Well, since he started to drive it he no longer parties as much as he used to. I really give him a lot of credit – he's doing quite well. I sometimes think I should start looking for something that actually brings some money.
- Stop it. Education is the basic thing. Look at your dad.
- Yes, but those were different times, Aneta. We are heading in totally different direction. Even large enterprises struggle. It is the small businesses and booths that make money.
- Not true, Mark. Little booths will not supply the entire country. Large enterprises, soon or later will have to face the difficulties and start to produce. In order to do so they need educated staff.
- You're right but I just don't want to wait doing nothing hoping that some day an opportunity will come for me to test my own self. Right now the situation is: a person wants to but is unable to. It has nothing to do with this or

that job. It's just the reality –
everything stopped.
- You are so grumpy today. It
will all get back on the right
track – Aneta finished.

Several dozens of people waited in lane to
get in the club "Musical One".
Andrzej pulled over at the parking lot, got out
of the car and came up to the door.
- Where do you think you're
going? Stay in lane like
everybody else – several
voices shouted.
Without paying any attention to these
protests he knocked at the door. They
opened and a man of humongous size stood
before him. He was way over two feet tall,
some 180 pounds and of an athletic built.
His nickname was "Yogi" on account of his
looks – he kind of looked like a grizzly bear.
His personality matched the outside as well.
He worked as a bouncer in various clubs and
had a reputation of being 100% effective,
meaning nobody could get inside without
him knowing about it.
- Hola, Andrzejek!
- How is it going, Yogi? Quite
busy in here, uh? Looks like
you won't be bored.
- As usual, nothing new. Get
in, quickly.
- Why is he getting in ahead of
everybody else? – Someone
yelled.

Yogi backed off a little bit, looked out to the crowd and screamed:

- Shut up or punch!

All of the sudden it got quiet. Yogi came in with Andrzej and the two of them sat at the bar.

- What can I get you? - asked the barmaid.
- Two whiskeys, "Pepsi" on the side and a pack of "Marlboro" – answered Andrzej.
- You're doing well, I hear, making all kind of dew on those trips through the country.
- I'm doing quite well but want to add radio and TV stuff to the rest.
- Where will you get it?
- I know some people here and there. I have two stereos lined up and the speakers. Next week there should be more.
- I envy you a bit, Andrzej. On the other hand I am glad though. It's always better to know people who have some than broke losers.
- I'm telling you, it's not easy. People are generally broke. They want to buy things but have nothing to buy it for. I have to run like crazy along the coast trying to sell something.

- Why don't you give it up and just go to Germany. I have some friends there. They would help you.
- I know, a lot of friends of mine also left – for Italy. They're waiting for Canada to accept them. Honestly, if I were to go abroad, I'd only go to the States. But I can't leave my mother, my brother and his wife.
- Get them all to go – Yogi insisted.
- Well, I'll wait and see what happens.

They talked a while longer and Yogi had to go back to his post. Andrzej mingled between tables greeting friends. He danced a bit as well and met a new girl doing so.

- I really enjoyed the dance – she said – but it is getting late and I really have to go back home.
- Oh, come on. We've only just begun. Besides, since when beautiful girls, like you, have to come home. As far as I remember it was always a gorgeous carriage that would wait for the princess – he said jokingly.

The girl turned visibly red.

- You're very sweet but I'm not a girl who easily falls into a guy's entrapment.

- So if I offered a glass of champagne you'd still consider me a hunter?
- No, I wouldn't – she said and they sat down
- What is your name?
- Marzena.
- I'm Andrzej. So, what are you doing here in Bydgoszcz?
- How do you know I'm not from the area?
- Because our local girls don't think of us as hunters setting up their traps – they both laughed.
- OK, ok, I'm sorry I prejudged you. I study fine arts here. What do you do?
- Me? – he thought for a second – I work with handicapped children.
- That must be interesting – her eyes lit up with interest – interesting job that pays well since you drink champagne and smoke "Marlboro".
- Oh, it is very interesting – Andrzej continued – I go to Switzerland often to participate in international seminars, exchange experiences, etc.
- Wow! Tell me more. This is the kind of job I've been dreaming about.

- See what a small world – a minute ago you were ready to go and now you want to stay out of your own free will.

They talked for a long time until closing time. Andrzej was coming up with the most unbelievable stories putting the girl in different moods. She laughed, cried, finally when they were finished he offered a ride home.

- Is this your cab?
- No, I borrowed it from my brother. My car is in a shop. If you want we can pop in to my friend's place. He lives around here.
- OK, but just for a minute.

He took her to he house of his driving buddy. He had a big apartment and lived alone so quite frequently this was a venue for various parties. They just made it to one of them now. Music, good alcohol and cigarettes suggested that Andrzej's friend was also doing well. Marzena was astonished by the selection of booze.

- How can he afford this?
- He owns a restaurant in Koszalin and lives in Bydgoszcz only because his mother, who is ill also lives here – he lied again.
- That's great he cares about his family so much.
- Oh yes, all of my friends are very good people – he embraced and kissed her. She

96

didn't protest and so he took
her to another room where
they ended up making love
passionately. Afterwards she
fell asleep. He got dressed
and left. A strange girl was in
the kitchen.

- - Do you have a car? – she
  asked.
- Yes, where do you need to get
  to?
- Wherever you want to take
  me.
- "It will be a tiresome night",
  he thought. They left and
  headed straight to the hotel.

- Do not get so anxious, Mr.
  Mark. First months always
  are difficult but it only gets
  better afterwards. This is
  typical after graduation.

- Before college they were
  telling me once I graduate I'll
  get on my own feet. Now it
  looks like it's quite the
  opposite. I don't expect
  miracles but I have to make
  more. I mean I have two
  children to feed and clothe.
- At this moment there is
  nothing I can do. Just go
  home and relax for now.
  We'll talk tomorrow. I'll see

if I can hook you up with
some extra work.
Mark left his boss' office irritated.
"You sweat for so many years; sleepless
nights, tough exam sessions. I counted so
much to settle well. Ania can walk already.
Jasiu will start any day. Time goes by so fast
and I'm stuck in the same place I started" –
thoughts were running through his head.
"What should I do? Should I quit this job
and take up – like Andrzej – a cab or private
booth on the black market? Was it worth
studying for so many years? On the other
hand had I not studied I wouldn't have
known what I'm losing. But what good does
it do to know. Doesn't change anything. I
have Masters degree and am making less than
a taxi driver. What a reality!"
He thought as he was walking. His father
always said: "Life is a book, but it's not a
book about you. You can only write a
chapter about yourself".
"… and you wish to leave a mark behind
you, no matter what. Lived on this earth,
lived dozens of years…" – words of a song
mingled with his thoughts.
"Well, it's time to write my own chapter" –
he said it to himself out loud.

-   Andrzej! – Mark shouted as
    soon as he walked into the
    house.
-   What is it?
-   Come here for a minute. I
    really need to speak with you.
They both sat down.

- You look like you just saw a ghost. What happened? – Andrzej said.
- Maybe I just saw a ghost of poverty and hunger.
- Well, tell me what's going on, OK?
- We're leaving! – Mark yelled.
- Where, when, how?
- We'll get to Italy and then to America.
- Those college years really got to you, huh? I mean it. Do you ever think about what you're saying? It's not like you can just drop a turd and then leave! – Andrzej was screaming.
- I know it sounds easier than it is to accomplish but I've made up my mind. I just wanted to know if you're going with me or not.

Andrzej was just sitting there. "The cab needs work, maybe even new engine. It will take several weeks. God knows how much they'll charge me and if they fix it enough to get it up and running for three, four years. I'm not going to get a new car – that's for sure. All it will be is patching the holes and fixing something every two months. Maybe he's right. Maybe it is worth a shot" – he stopped thinking for a minute and asked:
- Well, how do you imagine that?

99

- We'll sell the cab and what's
  in it – radio, meter, etc. We
  buy vacation package to
  Rome. Once we're there
  Michal will pick us up. We'll
  join a transition camp for a
  few months and finally fly to
  the States. So many people
  went through that and now
  they're happy.
- How much time do we need to
  get it all ready?
- I'd say two months, or so.
- That would mean we'd leave
  in the year 85'.
- Yup.

Andrzej opened a bottle of beer and drank it
at once.

- I'm going.

The two of them were joined by Aneta and
discussed details regarding the departure as
well as how to assure the financial security
for her and the kids. Mom didn't have muc
to say throughout this time and only
sometimes threw a question to which nobody
really had an answer. A week later they
started to put their plans to work. Surprise
for everybody – Mark took over the initiative
and took care of everything. Andrzej didn't
mind at all. He took his time to say goodbye
to his girls. When it came to say farewell to
their buddies there was no end to parties. It it
was only the mother's heart counting days
left to the big day. She knew they were
going in to unknown world. After all these
years of taking care of and upbringing her

son the time has come for them to leave her.
And although she knew there was nothing
wrong with it, hr heart cried inside.

Andrzej was holding on to his mother. Mark
was kissing the little ones: Ania and Jasio
promising they would soon be together again.
Ania was looking through luggage making
sure that they took everything they needed.
Just before leaving Mark and Andrzej were
looking carefully around the apartment, as if
they wanted to keep as much as possible in
their memory. They left and the silence took
over. Ticking of the clock seemed louder
than usually, counting the time of separation.
When they reached the "Okecie" airport it
was very cold.

- I could have worn long johns
  – Andrzej was upset.
- For what? You'll be in Rome
  in two hours – Mark replied.

Passport customs control went relatively
quickly and soon they were inside the
airplane. Mare looked through the window
and realized two streams of tears on his
cheek. He wasn't even trying to stop them.
"Why am I crying? I should feel happy. I'm
going to make my life better not worse", he
thought. And in his own thoughts he tried
hard to find some answer. His thoughts
evolved around his son and daughter, around
his wife and his mother. He realized though
that they were not the reasons he cried.
"I'm crying because of Poland! Yes, it's
because of her!"

101

Andrzej was looking at the flight attendant's
hands:

- You will meet a handsome
  blond guy who will change
  your life. You will be rich
  and happy. And...
- Excuse me – Mark interrupted
  – what is this gentleman doing
  with your palm?
- He is a fortune-teller and is on
  his way to Vatican City to
  meet the Pope – flight-
  attendant replied.

Mark busted out laughing.

Chapter III

Birches, oaks and evergreens – trees so close to our hearts. We grow up around them and look through them at each other almost every day. In the summer they overwhelm us with their beautiful green while in the wintertime they soothe us with their silence from underneath the white coat of the season. Pictures of lands with oranges and palms are strange and exotic and it is only through the eyes of imagination that we travel and visit those tropical climates. We enjoy the sunrays walking through the palm avenues. Mark was starting to realize that his dreams were coming true.

They landed in Rome. Italians working at the airport were running around; dark complexion and sunglasses were everywhere to be seen. Sun was strong pleasant at the same time giving the much desired sense of serenity.

Mark and Andrzej were walking through the airport in silence. They looked around with interest, as the way the airport looked was quite different from the one they had seen in Poland.

- Welcome o Rome! – they heard Michal's joyous greeting. They approached him and shook his hand sincerely.
- What are we doing now? – Andrzej began.

- Nothing yet. I will go with your group to the hotel and explain everything there.
- Michal, look at this palm tree! – Mark screamed, as this was the first palm tree in Italy he saw. After a while he realized this was nothing new for Michal who had been in Italy for the past three months.

Small, modestly decorated hotel room had a lot of charm to it. First of all this was ROME, and its window was right onto the street.
Mark was looking through it watching pedestrians and cars pass by. Life seemed to him to be so different here. He was observing people crossing the street on the red lightwhile the cars coming would stop and let them reach the opposite side of the street with no hassle.
"That is something. At home everyone would scream and yell at each other by now", he thought.
In the middle of the room sitting at the table Andrzej and Michal were planning the way to the refugee camp.
- Today we'll stay here in the hotel. You paid for it and besides it is late already and before we get to "Latina" it would be evening. The offices will be closed by then.

- We can spend a night here but tomorrow we're getting out of here – Michal replied.
- Tell us Michal, what are we going to do, you know – when we get there.
- You are all set. I took care of everything there. You will sleep in a barrack. The camp is overloaded and if they see an empty place they right away put someone on it. As soon as we get there I will take your luggage while you go to register in the office. They will take your passports. Then you will get shaving stuff and tooth brushes.
- What about the papers to get to U.S.? – Mark kept asking.
- This will come later and I will explain that to you too.

The three of them sat at the table and opened a bottle of "ZYTNIA", reminiscing old times in Poland. The next morning, after breakfast, Mark went to the trip manager.

- Good morning.
- Hallo – the woman answered with a smile – What can I do for you, Mr. Mark?
- I just came to say good-bye.

She looked at him with understanding.

- You're staying too, huh?
- What you mean "you too"?

- It means that from all of our group there will be only few people to come back home
- My brother is staying too.
- I knew from the very beginning what was going on. Your friend awaited you at the airport and then slept in your room. This is not my first trip – she continued with pride – and regardless, I'm wishing you all the best.

Mark hugged her sincerely and walked out.

- So, how did it go? – Andrzej asked.
- Very well, not a problem.

Miles south of Rome is the city of Latina, surrounded by mountain orange fields on one side and by the golden beach on the other. Nobody really knew much about the origin of the name. Was it named after some woman or maybe meant something like "Latin". One thing though that every scavenger from Europe knew about it was that it meant "Future".

The camp was located almost in the center of the city. It was surrounded by a short wall and had a decorative gate up front. The barrack formed a half-circle and were named alphabetically from letter A to H. In the middle of the camp was the administrative building and in one corner was cafeteria and church. Andrzej was looking around curiously.

- It looks like military base – he said.
- Because that's what it was before – I heard.
- It's not bad, though.

They walked into the building H.

- I'm sorry, my bad – Andrzej changed his mind once he saw inside of the building. Its walls were covered partially with blood and wine stains, and partially with paint. There was glass on the floor – a lot of it - and no locks in the door that had partial frames.
- What happened here? War broke out or what? – Andrzej asked. Michal was standing next to him laughing.
- This is the every day reality – he said.

They all came inside where everybody was already waiting for the newcomers. A little chaos happened once everyone started to scream their names at once. At the end people found their seats and began telling their immigrant stories. One left Poland through the Czech border, the other one came from Sweden on a fake passport – there was no end to the stories, which lasted till the morning.

- Your name and date of birth – a woman said in Italian.

Mark looked at her with surprise not understanding anything.

- Do you speak English? – she asked now.
- No – Mark answered.
- How about Russian? - she now asked in Russian?

Now he felt more like at home. He knew Russian quite well and burden fell of his shoulders. He started answering in Russian:

- Yes.

Once they finished filling out all the papers he thanked her and finally left. He laughed to himself thinking: "I would have never thought that Russian would be useful in trying to get to America through Italy". Andrzej was right after him. Once he saw an attractive woman he right away started in German. She answered – they found a common language. He spoke German well and so there were no problems with filling out his papers. Strange woman flattered by his complements gave him many priceless advices concerning the future. Afterwards the boys stood up for a photo and soon they were given green, three-part booklets.

- Now you guys are full blown immigrants – Michal said.
- What you mean, "full blown"?
- You have your "profugies". The green papers you hold – we call them "profugies". They are temporary Italian ID's.
- We have to toast to it! Let's get some wine – Andrzej offered. Mark enthusiastically agreed – We'll get the most

109

popular camp wine,
"Lambrusko". You have three
"milaks"? – Mark didn't
understand.

- Three what?
- "Milak" – meaning tree grand
Italian. "Uno mile lire" means
a grand, "de mile lire" –two
grand, then tre, quarto, etc. In
other words "milak" is a
thousand in this Polish-Italian
slang.

They walked into a store and bought two
bottles of wine.

- You know what, two bottles
for three grand that's cheap. I
saw a bottle of mineral water
go for a thousand. How do
people live here?

They were wandering through the streets and
finally sat in a park "Piazza Popolo". The
watched as the people were passing by. The
square was in the middle of the town
surrounded with colorful building. During
the day it was a typical shopping area while
at night a popular gathering place.
Interesting characteristics of the place were
its BOBKOWE trees with lawrence leaves –
popular condiment in Poland.
They were sipping the wine talking about
politics and sharing their impressions of
what's around them. Tired of talking they
made one tour around the square looking at
store vintages full of merchandise. Radio
and TV equipment, fashionable clothes, guns
and pocketknives – stores looked very

different than what they were used to in the old country. They weren't quite sure how to handle this – should they be happy to se it all now or regret the years spent on watching empty shelves of the stores at home? All the colorful wonders were within the reach of their hands now. There was just one thing separating those who watch from those who buy – money.

- How much money we have? – Mark asked.
- Two hundred dollars; t should last till we leave for the States if we manage to do so within the next two months – Andrzej answered and continued – If not it will be tough. We'll worry about it later. We can afford a few small things now.
- Here it goes – Mark mumbled.
- Well, what do you think? Do we have to continue looking like discarded remnants of socialism? A pair of pants and some nice shirt won't hurt, and a pair of sunglasses of course. At least people won't give us a look anymore – Andrzej argued.
- That's not what this is about. You want the chicks to start giving you a look – a different one though.
- Well, that two. But you have to understand my brother that right now we are the

representatives of our country and the ambassadors of the friendly relations between our two nations – Italy and Poland.

- Stop the BS. Just admit that it's about you wanting to be a charmer.
- OK, so we have to buy some clothes so that I can get a hot Italian girl – does that satisfy you, Sir? – Andrzej got impatient.
- Of course it does – Mark answered jokingly and they both laughed.
- We'll do some shopping tomorrow.

Life in the camp had its own routine. Breakfast: soup, noodles and bread. Lunch: soup, noodles and bread. Dinner: soup, noodles and bread. Meanwhile people were checking out the bulletin board where names of people were listed. They were names of those who soon were to leave for countries of their choice. The main square resounded with conversations about Canada, U.S. and Australia. Multilingual Babel Tower was alive as ever. There were funny situations too, when people from different countries tried to communicate with each other. Hungarians, Poles, Romanians, Czechs, Albanians, Yugoslavians – were talking their hands out. But there were also signs of common understanding as names of socialist leaders were thrown: Jaruzelski, Kadar, Ceaucescu – all of them formed the unwritten dialog of mutual understanding just as much as disgust with the system and perspective of the better future. What was prevailing? It was hard to tell since people were choosing to leave their countries for different reasons. The camp was also home for regular criminals for whom this was the only way out of potential trouble. Thieves were looking for an opportunity to make better money. Families were sharing their dreams about the better life. Disappointed idealists abandoned their socialist wealth and traded it into the capitalist poverty. Many patriotic things were said but the sense of patriotism per se was nowhere to be found.

- Mark, we have to start learning English – Andrzej said at some point.
- You're right. We have to or we'll end up in trouble once in the U.S. They do have English courses here.
- We could sign up next week.
- Good idea. Tell me, don't you miss Poland?
- Honestly, not really. I do miss Aneta and the kids but nothing besides that. I'm actually surprised by it myself. What about you?
- I don't think I miss it. But I can't get used to being broke. Overall I always had the

money to catch a cab in Bydgoszcz. Here all I can do is just watch.

- Andrzej, what do you expect – to become a millionaire in a month? There will come the time for everything. Besides you already are a millionaire – just convert the dollars you have into the Italian money.
- Your sense of humor really got sharp here in Italy, didn't it? I keep thinking about those who are here with entire families – these little kids have no clue where they're at or where they're going.
- It's true now, but wait until they grow up in Canada or the States – they will thank their parents for what they did.
- Politics has noting to do with these people. They're not here because they disagree with socialism. They are looking after their own skin, want to do better in life and give their kids a better chance. Socialism shouldn't count them as run-aways rather. It made them leave their homes, families and friends.

Evenings in the camp were also somewhat routine. Drunken nights, singing and yelling were an everyday reality. Women were running away from drunken men to avoid

114

rape. Sounds of the door being broken into were the testimony that groups thieves stayed busy as well. Personal fights often evolved into international conflicts involving the use of bats and knives. A great deal of self-determination and character was very much needed in order not to go crazy. Some people simply locked themselves in their rooms – they didn't feel like participating in this "nightlife" full of partying and fights. Some prayed that God gets them out of their nightmare. Even the most intense of prayers were interrupted by the sounds of bottles thrown on concrete and walls. What is it that wakes in us the wildest of instincts? Is it the desire to impress somebody or perhaps the internal weakness? Months of waiting mixed with dreams about the better future made people feel frustrated and disappointed. Add to it lack of speaking the language and the very different way of life to the one they had gotten used to for years and you have a recipe for book model of depression. This was the natural selection – some of the unfortunate campers ended up in jail, others were deported while still some decided to go back to their home countries on their own. Andrzej was sitting at the table playing cards.

- Turn it up a little – he said to the boy sitting by the TV.
- OK. It's called "The Perfect Stranger" by Deep Purple.
- I know. I love this song – Andrzej answered.
- Is there any wine left? – asked done of the players.

- I've got one spare bottle –
  Andrzej answered.
- Well, open it up. Really hot
  out here today – the second
  player added.

Andrzej digged out the bottle from
underneath the bed and placed on the table.
They opened it up quickly and poured.

- Jasio, I think you better stop.
  You're already pretty buzzed.
- So what?
- I'm just saying you're pretty
  plastered already so how are
  you going to keep playing?
- Don't worry about that, ok? –
  Jasio answered and dunked
  the whole glass at once. As
  soon as he finished all of the
  sudden he screamed:
- The window!!!

Andrzej rushed up and forced the window up.
A stream of red liquid traveled from the table
to the window. Jasio threw up without even
moving. He wiped his mouth and asked:

- So, are we playing or what?
- I've never seen anyone puke
  like that before – Andrzej
  simply stated.
- It took practice to come to
  perfection – Jasio answered
  with pride.
- You know, sometimes when I
  look at you I can't help but
  thinking you're like "gorski"
  /mountain-like/

116

- You mean the coach of the
  soccer team?
- No, I mean dumb as a
  mountain sheep.

Everyone started to laugh only Jasio reached
out for his ax, which he kept under his bed
and started chasing Andrzej. They ran for a
while and finally Jasio said:

- Ok, I'm not mad anymore.
  Let's just keep playing.

They sat again as if nothing happened and
kept playing.

- I'm fed up with this
  whorehouse, Mark. I have my
  wife and children in Poland. I
  had a dream that my children
  didn't recognize me when
  they saw me and addressed me
  as "Mr." It's only been three
  months. What's gonna
  happen next?
- Do you have a lot of cash in
  Poland? – Mark asked.
- Are you crazy? I have
  nothing.
- Then simmer down. Your
  wife and your kids are
  counting on you, that you'll
  make it and eventually get the
  over as well, that you will live
  like a normal family for once.
  This isn't some punishment
  for you to be here. You can
  always go back but if you do
  so in a month you'll go back
  to the same problems, which

made you, leave in the first
place. Then you'll want to try
again except you wouldn't be
able to anymore and then what
you're gonna do? Have you
heard about "immigrant's
dreams"?

- No.
- You got to Poland, meet your
friends, make love to your
wife and play with your kids.
You go out to eat, party. Your
family is now jealous, as are
your buddies, and everything
is just beautiful. But then you
want to come back but you
can't. The borders are closed.
Cops take away your passport.
You wake up sweaty looking
around – you realize you're
still in the camp, and you feel
relieved. You've never
dreamt anything like this?

- No.
- Well, soon or later you will.
You probably haven't gotten
there yet. Stop worrying.
You should be up for
departure soon. Take frequent
walks and watch TV. Study
English. Try to kill time and
you'll see – everything will
work out – Mark finished.

- You're right. I'll try to do as
you say. Thanks a lot my
man.

But after one week Mark found out that his friend from Krakow came back to Poland.

- How much for this shirt? – Andrzej asked. An Albanian guy answered with mixture of Polish, Russian and Italian;
- 2000 lires, just for you.
- OK, give me two. Do you have pants too?
- No pants, no. Wine – yes, want?
- Give me the wine.

The Albanian opened up the wine, poured into glasses and handed Andrzej the guitar.

- You play, guitar you play. You play good.

Andrzej started to play. Sometimes they were sipping on the wine and talked the Polish-Albanian gibberish. Mark entered the room. They were both smoking and singing. He came up to Andrzej and whispered:

- What to hell are you doing with this thief?

The Albanian heard it, came up to Mark and said:

- Mark, you not be mad. I no steal from Andrzej and Mark.

Now all three of them sat down and Mark listened to the Albanian guy's story. It was his 5th time here in Latina. He was entering Italy illegally as much as it was possible, changing name each time. His goal was to manage staying as long as possible before the Italians figure out that it's the same person. Meanwhile he was stealing whatever he could and selling it in the camp. The money he made he was sending to his family in Albania. No country would accept him, as he was a convict. They wouldn't put him in jail either because he "didn't steal enough". So he just kept being deported and coming back. He treated it as his job. Mark started to feel sympathetic thinking, "Poor guy, life made him a professional pocket thief. Who will I become in America? What if I can't find a job? What if I end up stealing myself?" Question just kept coming up but he didn't even try to find answers.

Education, tradition and ideals of romanticism form our existence. And so we think sometimes about ourselves as of some models knowing how and what about everything. We try to follow in footsteps of the characters from books. It is so welcome in our country. But, one life throws us to lands far away we are forced to rethink the old values and come to the right conclusions anew. The Italian reality has not accepted our own Wolodyjowskis or Kmicices. And it was not because of some bias or prejudice. It was simply the differences of cultures that made many young immigrants abandon the old habits or stereotypical behaviors. For some it was just a matter of time, for others something impossible to accomplish.

> - I bought some sausage. Do you want some? – Andrzej asked.

120

- Silly question, sure I do –
  Mark answered.

Andrzej divided the sausage and out it on two plated. They ate in silence. Finally Andrzej started:

- You know what? There is an opportunity to work a little bit on the grap.e fields. Do you want to go?
- That's not a bad idea. We'd make some money.
- They pay 15000 for six hours. It's not much but always something that will cover food and cigarettes. That should even be enough to get the beer. I don't think it's such hard work considering how little they're offering. It won't hurt to try.

Jasio entered the room.

- Hi guys. What's cooking?
- We just got some sausage – Mark answered.
- I see, but I also see some bullion here.

The brothers looked at each other puzzled since there was no bullion. Jasio meanwhile came up to the stove and poured some "bullion" to a cup. It turned out that the bullion was simply water, in which they had cooked the sausage. The brothers sat quietly.

- You don't mind me having some of this, do you?
- No, not at all.

- It needs some salt and pepper
  – Jasio continued and added
  the aforementioned
  condiments – others than that
  it's delicious.

Andrzej thought: "What a moron". Jasio
drank up, thanked them and left.

A stocky Italian guy drove up to the "post" as
the campers used to call the spot from which
volunteers to work formed a lane. A dozen
men or so hopped into the bus. Trip wasn't
long, half an hour if even that. People got
out of the vehicle and looked at the fields of
grapes. These were the never-ending fields
and they will remember them for years to
come.

- What do they give away? –
  Andrzej asked.
- Stuff to dig with – said Mark.
- So short? We're tall, need
  longer ones.
- I'm sure they have them.

But it turned out that they didn't and
everybody received the same equipment.

- Damn, these are good to play
  with but not to work with! –
  Andrzej was unhappy.
- Quit your whining. It'll work
  out somehow.

They started to dig. Mark had a lot of
enthusiasm and soon was way ahead of the
others.

- What's wrong with you?
  You've go a motor up your
  butt or what? Slow down a

122

little or the Italian will think
you're the only one working
for real.

- Don't worry, once I finish
with this one here I'll tae a
break and sit under the tree.

The whether was great; blue sky, gentle
smooches of the wind and lots of sun. In
spite of what one might thing the soil was
neither moist nor soft. In fact it was hard as a
rock. Mark was red and sweaty once he
reached the end of his GRZADKA. "Finally
I'll catch a break", he thought. Not a minute
went by when the stocky Italian came up to
him.

- Bene Polako, bene Polako –
he said, which meant "good
Pole". He led Mark to the
second GRZEDA and told
him to start right away. Mark
was trying to tell him that he's
had enough of grapes for now
but the Italian didn't even try
to listen and walked away.
"Well, here's my capitalism. I
should have listened to
Andrzej", he thought. At the
end of the day everybody sat
near the bus. Arms burnt by
the sun and pimples breaking
on the hands gave proof that
the work they were doing
could not really be considered
as light. Some people got the
heat stroke, others fainted due
to exhaustion and dehydration.

When they came back to the
gates of camp they breathed
relieved.
- So, that would be it as for the
hard work in Italy, huh? –
Andrzej said summarizing the
day. Mark laughed and
answered:
- You're right. We ought to do
what we like in life.
- That's exactly it, and I like
making cash so I'll keep
making cash.
"Always the same", Mark thought.

Andrzej woke up and looked around the
room. This was not the camp room anymore,
though. He saw a naked girl right next to
him. She was Italian, black air to the
shoulders, healthy tanned complexion mad
Andrzej feel good.
"Lucky me to have finished with her and not
the other one. That one was married. If her
husband caught us I'd have been dead", he
thought. The girl woke up and hugged
Andrzej with a smile. He held her closely
and caressed her hair looking straight into her
eyes. Beautiful black eyes with long lashes
surrounded by carefully made up eyebrows
made him feel like he was holding in his
arms an Egyptian queen. "Cleopatra", he
thought – "This is what she must have looked
like". He touched her face and her breasts
trying to absorb the wonderful view. He
caressed her thighs just in order to finally
enter her body with indescribable joy and full

124

respect. Sun gently laid its rays on their entangled bodies.

"Andrzej Polskowicz", "Mark Polskowicz" – names on the list kept Mark's attention.

- At last! - he screamed and rushed towards the barracks.
- Andrzej! Andrzej! - he kept yelling as he finally got to their room – We're signed up on the list to the American embassy!

Andrzej jumped and embraced Mark as both of them celebrated.

Visits to the embassies were the breaking points in immigrants' lives. Their outcome was crucial as it determined whether the person met all the requirements to qualify for the permanent residency. Sometimes people who would be considered well rounded and sincere were denied while crazy druggies were permitted to emigrate.

Mark and Andrzej came to the U.S. embassy on time and dressed appropriately – suit and tie.

- Polskowicz – their name was said. Mark and Andrzej looked at each other thinking "Which one of us?" Finally decided:
- Let's both go.

At the very beginning they were put under oath and asked whether they needed an interpreter. They said "no". Consul asked them about names of their parents, schools they attended, etc. He asked Mark how are his wife and children and at the end asked Andrzej what was he going to do in the United States. Andrzej answered, "make money". As they left Mark screamed at him in anger:

- Why did you have to answer in such a stupid way?
- It wasn't stupid. What was I supposed to say that I'll be a good boy and go to church every Sunday?
- No, you could have simply said that you'd try to find job in your field or something like this.
- Mark, why do you always want to say things because they – according to you – are "appropriate? They don't know you, know nothing about you - how you feel, what you think, what can you afford. They spent 10 minutes with us – that's all.
- So what that it was only 10 minutes? We represent Poland.
- Not true – Andrzej contested – for them Poland is a part of the communist block represented by communist government. For Americans we are nothing but people who fled Poland. We represent ourselves and ourselves alone.

Mark kept quiet. He didn't want to listen to his brother's argument. It was impossible for him to comprehend that years spent on studying, hundreds of books read and nights of discussions all. Of the sudden were worthless. "He's wrong – he thought – there are other values aside from money left in this world".

Time in the camp was passing by fast. Friends were saying farewell to friends as they were preparing for their journeys. At the same time the newcomers were being welcomed. Two brothers decided to use the reminding time wisely; Mark started to attend the English course, visited the city as well as the surrounding area while Andrzej kept playing cards, drinking wine and chasing girls.

Mark left the school and was walking up to the bulletin board. By the small square in between the buildings several men approached him.

- Hey, blondie! – one of them yelled – light me up some smoke here.

Mark has seen them before and heard of them. Those were the "neo-nazis"; most of the time drunk and marching through the camp singing nazi songs. Whoever got in their way usually got into trouble; they stole and raped, and got away with everything.

- I don't have cigarettes on me – Mark answered.

- Then give us your money and we'll buy them ourselves- the thug answered with a smirk.
- Try to make money on your own and you'll see how easy it is – as Mark finished his answer he felt a punch. One, two – he stopped counting. He "woke up" after a while feeling terribly. He couldn't open his left eye. His knees and elbows were swollen and there was blood on his face. He got himself together and finally came to his room.
- What happened to you? – Andrzej asked and tried to be funny – Did you have an encounter with a car or what?
- The fascists fucked me up right around the block.

Andrzej got up without saying a word, grabbed his military belt and rolled it aroundhis fist.

- Jasio, get you ax and Karol you get the bat.

They left.

After an hour the Italian police arrived to the camp. Some were looking for those "who did it" while the ambulances were helping out the victims. "What happened?" – everyone whispered. Mark was standing at the gate looking at faces of the victims being put into ambulances. All of them were the ones who had attacked him.

128

"Hi did them good", he thought about
Andrzej.

After this incident number of rumors broke
out in the camp; "Mafia" – some thought
while other were saying "Russian KGB", etc,
etc. And only Andrzej, Jasio and Karol were
sitting in their room drinking wine and
pretending to be surprised.

- What a dangerous country,
  Italy – Jasio said.
- You have to be really careful
  – Karol chipped in.
- Beast thing is to leave as soon
  as possible – Andrzej
  summarized.

The doctor's clinic was full of patients.
Before departure from Italy everyone had to
go through medical exam. Andrzej was
sitting at the very end. Mark has already left.
A beautiful girl walked in, which Andrzej
noticed right away and offered his chair.

- I'm Andrzej.
- Grazyna – she answered.
- Listen, how would you like to
  be my wife?

She looked at him as if he were an exotic pet.

- Are you feeling all right?
- What am I saying, geez? I
  was just thinking that they let
  the married couples go first so
  if I said that you were my
  wife, they would take us right
  away and we'd both save
  about 2 – 3 hours.

- Oh, I see. I guess that'll be fine.
- Cool. So you wait for me here and I'll go and take care of things.

And so he left. After a while he gave her a sign and both of them walked into the office. A nurse gave them the paperwork to fill out.

- Now it's gonna suck – Grazyna said – they'll see we have different names.

She was right. The nurse took their forms and came back right after a minute asking about their last names and why are they different. Andrzej had the situation under control, however, and explained how hard it was for a married couple to leave Poland hence they decided to keep their names separate. They got married here, in Italy, but their documents still aren't ready. The nurse believed him, walked them intor the room and told them both to undress.

- So, what's it gonna be now? – Grazyna asked.
- Get undressed; I won't look – Andrzej answered.
- You must be crazy or something. We've known each other for 10 minutes and you want me to parade in front of you butt naked already?
- Why not. What do you think I'm supposed to do?

They both busted out laughing.

130

- I've never met anybody as
  fucked up as you? – she stated
  calmly.
- Neither have I.

They saw the doctor in two separate rooms,
however, and once they left they headed
straight to the camp. After traditional glass
of wine and brief conversation about
America they both came to conclusion that
it's about time to consummate their new
"marriage". In other words this was their
"wedding night".

Knock on the door woke Andrzej and
Grazyna up.

- Come in – she said. Mark
  stood at the door:
- I'm sorry to just interrupt your
  sleep like this, but I need to
  speak with my brother.
- I have nothing to hide room
  my wife – Andrzej said
  jokingly.
- What's wrong with him now?
  – Mark asked Grazyna.
- Oh, just don't pay attention to
  him. He's been like this since
  yesterday – she said with a
  smile.
- OK, well doesn't matter, I
  guess. Hey, bro listen up –
  we're on the list. We're
  leaving for Rome tomorrow.
  We've got to start packing so
  you better get up.

Andrzej jumped out of bed, dressed and
kissed Grazyna "good-bye", saying: "I'll see

131

you soon my beloved. Wait for me and be faithful". Afterwards they left.

- What are you talking about? What wife, what's the "wait for me" about? You're really on something.
- Chill out, bro. I'm just saying stuff out of happiness, but it's all-good. Farewell Latina! Welcome Rome!

History mixed with the present; thousands of cars and passengers getting through the narrow streets, lines of Roman Legions, people working as slaves, charming women – here is the crowd from all over the world thrown in the panorama of Rome. So many thoughts and pictures were running through Mark's mind. Rome is a very different kind of city. It is the place where past collides with the present making it all a well functioning organism. While looking at the Coliseum the thoughts of gladiators in their bloody fight as well as the general sense of the Cesar's era are ever-present. A moment later you step on the street and lines of cars automatically get you into the 20th century. Small buss sped through the city, as Mark and Andrzej were sitting and just absorbing what was going on around them. They found themselves on a wide road Via Nomentana and after a short time stopped in front of the hotel called "World". It was a very cozy place sitting on a hill and surrounded by gardens, far away from the noise of the traffic and the whole city life. Some employees of

the hotel were staring at the newcomers
hungry for memories. Everyone was in
excellent mood and the hotel looked nothing
liked the camp they all remembered.
Mark was out on the balcony thinking: "What
are the kids doing? Do they still remember
me? Was it all worth it? It's all nice n'
dandy now – beautiful town, history all
around, nice hotel – but what's going to
happen later? I'm gonna have to find a job –
what will it be? When will Aneta and the
kids able to come? It's easier to make it once
you're alone but when you have the entire
family to feed – what then? Do they need
zoo-technologists there? Are dreamers like
me able to survive? Will I have to do
physical labor and hate what I'm doing?
What's mom going to do – all alone?"
Questions were pouring one after another.
We're never ready to answer them all.
Answer to one only brings about another.
"It's killing me – he continued thinking – I
guess I have reprogram my way of thinking.
It's no longer going to be "why?" but "how?"
Yes, life places us before various situations
and it's better to think how to solve them
then why did they even happen".

- Twenty!
- Nope, thirty!
- That's much; I'll give you
  twenty.
- Twenty-five!
Polish language was head all over. Andrzej
met a Polish tourist on one of the markets in
Rome. After official introduction and

random conversation on current events in Poland and Italy they got to the business. Andrzej was a frequent visitor of the markets and there were tons of them in Rome. His favorite one was by the train station Termini, the other one closer to the Vatican City. He often ran into Poles who came down here with tourist groups. He used to buy anything that's useful from them; cameras, crystals, fur. Then he would sell it to the Italians. He truly enjoyed doing this and it was a profitable business to do – he could afford to visit Rome and got to see a lot; historical stuff as well as cafes and restaurants.

"Perhaps he should stay here, in Italy – Andrzej thought again – I'll apply for asylum and open up a small business. Italians are nice and it's good to do business with them. But what would Mark say? LIR is not as strong as the dollar is. If I stayed – would I regret later? Better stick to your first decisions. Why am I even thinking so much? …"

He was sitting on the "Spanish stairs" analyzing all possible scenarios and just occasionally stared at the tourists pass by. In the midst of this session of deep thinking a girl's voice brought him back on earth:

- How could you let them get your money?
- Can I help you with anything? – Andrzej asked. The couple paused and looked towards him.
- Are you from Poland?
- Yes.

- Tell us how to get in touch
  with the police here?
- What happened?
- I'll explain it to him – the guy
  said – We were walking down
  the street and stopped by the
  ice cream parlor. As the clerk
  was giving us the change I
  moved all the money to my
  shirt pocket so that it doesn't
  sit in my pants (I heard that
  the really good ones here even
  get to your side pockets). So,
  out of nowhere a bunch of
  kids ran out who basically
  started to tell us what a cute
  couple we are and that Agata
  must be the most beautiful
  girls on the planet. It kind of
  made us feel good and so we
  chatted with the kids for
  maybe a minute. As they
  were walking away I reached
  out to my pocket to give them
  some change for an ice cream
  and… nothing, all of the
  money just disappeared.
- How much have you lost? –
  Andrzej asked.
- Mye 20 dollars or so – the guy
  replied.
- And so what, you're going to
  go to the cops and tell them
  that some children stole your
  money?

135

-   Well, sure. It is a crime isn't
    it?
-   First of all don't expect that
    the cops will start a police
    chase after some kids that you
    can't even describe. And the
    second thing is don't make a
    fool out of yourself by telling
    that children ripped you of.
    Just consider this part of your
    trip expenses.
-   But those were the last bucks
    I've had – the guy couldn't get
    over his loss. Andrzej looked
    at him and felt sorry.
-   If you don't have any more
    I'll chip in.

The girl looked at Andrzej and said:

-   Are you like a good angel or
    you're just up for something
    here with us?

He looked at her with a smile.

-   None of the above. But I will
    invite you additionally for a
    glass of wine.

The three started to walk led by Andrzej.
They introduced themselves to each other
and Andrzej told them some stories about
Rome. The guy's name was Roman ad
talked about how hard he worked in order to
make ends meet. Agata kept quiet and just
looked at store windows and advertising
posters. At some point Roman asked:

-   Now what are you doing in
    Rome?

- I'm waiting to leave for the United States.

They sat down at the table and ordered some wine.

- Why do you want to go to America? You can make money in Poland just as well as in America. I go sometimes to Germany, to France – I make tons of money. I have a small store in Poland and sell whatever I bring from abroad.

They ordered another bottle and the more they drank the more open Roman was. He indeed had a store and does business abroad doing quite well. It also turned out that Agata was not his girlfriend but someone he met during the trip. At the end he pulled out a $50 bill and paid the tab. "What a pig – Andrzej thought – first he tricked me how broke he was and took my twenty and now it turned out to be a lie". Agata felt a little uneasy as she saw Roman paying. He meanwhile continued:

- Only losers leave Poland – the ones who can't make it there on their own.

Andrzej thought, "Now, that's too much". He got up from the table and approached the waiter on the side. When he came back he announced:

- I ordered some music for us so they will come up to us to sing in a minute.

137

The musicians indeed came up and sang. Andrzej ordered another bottle of wine.

- To the rich people from Poland! – he exclaimed raising toast pointing at Roman. They had a great time. Roman got drunk and blacked out eventually. Andrzej picked him up and packed into the taxicab. After a while they came back and Andrzej sat next to Agata.
- I don't understand you – he cheated you and me too by the way so why are you so good?
- Well, you see my dear; in life you sometimes lose and sometimes win. I've lost twenty bucks on account of this idiot but I've gained you. I do have to admit that I really spent a very nice evening with you.

He reached out for her hand and kissed it. She said:

- I only felt the beauty of Rome now. Such a shame I have to go back in just two days.

As they were talking a handsome Italian guy approached them and handed something to Andrzej.

- Two hundred; that's all he had – he whispered.
- Thank you. We'll strengthen everything out tomorrow.
- Who was it? – Agata asked.

- Oh, just a friend – Andrzej
answered with a smile. He did
not want to ruin the pleasant
atmosphere. The "friend" was
a local thief. Through a waiter
Andrzej let him know that a
guy with cash was sitting next
to him. He didn't know
though when and how did they
get Roman's cash. He opened
the small package and counted
exactly 200 dollars.
- Let's go dancing somewhere –
he said to Agata.

And so they went. At the door to the club
bouncers were checking hands and arms of
those who wanted to get in.

- What are they doing? – Agata
asked.
- They're just checking if you
don't have some tattoos.
- Gosh, I would never think.
Why?
- They don't like tattoos much
around here. They associate
them with criminal past.

They entered. The place was largely
attended by the Finnish and Dutch nationals.
The party was great and Andrzej had an
opportunity to show off is language skills.
He spoke Italian while at the bar or Russian
with the ones from Finland and English or
German with the Dutch.

- Look at you, Mr. Polyglot –
Agata said jokingly.

- I'm trying. The world seems brighter when you can talk to people.
- Why are you going so far away, Andrzej? You're smart, you're intellingent, you speak languages. You would be of such use in Poland.
- Please, don't start. Thinking is too much sometimes for me. I've made my decision and I'll see what happens.
- I didn't mean to hurt your feelings, just that emigrants always seemed like a different kind of people.
- That's how it used to be but now is time for the new generation.

They danced together in a deep embrace.

- I'm not sure how I'll be able to find you – Agata continued – I don't have your address and even you still don't know where in the States you're heading. I don't even know what's your last name... I don't wat this night to end. – she talked while a string of tear started to wash her cheek.
- Maybe that's how it was meant to be, and maybe it is for the better – Andrzej whispered in reply. He then thought: I have alwaysloved all of my girls, but they

140

wanted to have me just for themselves. They would stop me on my route, which in fact I haven't stared yet. It's hard to part while kissing but it's even worse to interrupt destiny. What is this destiny of mine?

- Can I spend the night? – Agata snapped him out of his thoughts.
- Sure, thanks for being first to ask. I don't know why but I just felt somewhat shy all of the sudden.

Agata stared at him hoping she would hold on to this evening and hold on to him – the boy from Rome.

In a park near the hotel the boys were playing soccer. It was an international match: Poland vs. Romania. The emigrants fought forcefully for the victory. The girls were cheering. Even the Italians passing by stopped on their ways to watch for a moment those efforts of the players. Italy is known for its love for soccer and sometimes there were more Italian fans witnessing those games than the fans from the hotel itself. There was a somewhat unexpected obstacle for the players – a tree growing right in the middle of the park soccer field. Potentially dangerous plays and passing often ended with nothing due to the activity of this natural defender. Mark was running against the net while suddenly a Romanian snatched the ball. Right now the way to the Polish net was wide open. The guy started to sprint vigorously. In the midst of this play he apparently failed to notice that he was running right toward the tree. Mark yelled: "Watch out! Watch out for the tree!" But the Romanian guy either couldn't or didn't want to hear him as he kept running. The game was tied at that time and the situation provided an opportunity to break it. A thump and moaning cut off the dream about victory. The guy fell down. Who knows how many constellations were up there in the sky? One thing was certain: the stars captured his dreams about soccer career.

- Is he alive? – the girls whispered.
- Yes – one of the Romanians answered.

The injured player got up after a while and headed to the hotel but not in a confident manner. Mark talked to him for a minute and returned to the field. The matched ended with a tie. In the evening while sitting on the balcony with friends Mark told the story of the day.

- So he snatches the ball and runs. I scream, "watch out for the tree" but he was like whatever. Then bang! He was gone.

Everybody laughed at his story. Mark continued:

- After the game he told me he could hear me yell but couldn't understand what I was screaming. What's the conclusion of this story? Knowing languages can save lives.

142

Andrzej listened to him also amused and at
the same time served the people his alcoholic
mixture. They praised it highly presenting a
grim on their faces at the same time.

- What's in it?
- OK, I'll tell you if you want to
  know so bad.

Andrzej reached to his bag and showed
empty bottles of spiritus and pineapple juice.

- Wow! Where did you get the
  spiritus? – everybody asked.
- Don't be mad. I have to tell
  you it is used here for
  somewhat different purpose
  than in Poland.
- Don't go around the bush.
  Just tell us.
- OK, so they use it here in
  small camping cooking
  machines – Andrzej said

swearing that there are no chemicals in it.
The boys looked at each other in silence and
after a while demanded: "If it's healthy, pour
us some more!" A housekeeper came up to
them and asked with a smile what were they
drinking. Andrzej told her it was an old
Polish liquor good for both body and mind.

- Can I try it?
- Sure thing! – Andrzej passed
  her a glass. The girl grabbed
  it and started to

drink: one LYK, two… She stopped, looked
at Andrzej as if she wanted to say something
but she couldn't. She ran out of the balcony
and took the staircase downstairs. After a
while she came back with the hotel manager.

143

What a conundrum – an accusation came out that they wanted to poison an employee. The situation was cleared when the empowered mind of the housekeeper asked for another portion of the "poison". It cheered them all up including the manager who ultimately tried the magical elixir himself.

Evenings on the balcony were passing one after another. It is easier to spend time with those who freely shared one common goal. Looking at life we often lose ourselves in our achievements. We start with school, go through our jobs, families continuously coming up with new challenges, and each one of them more difficult than the previous one. Meanwhile, however, we lose what's really important in life – the sense of pleasure. Every day of our life is an achievement on its own. The sooner we understand it the better for us. Emigrants are its perfect example. They left their homes, cars, and property with one goal only – the "new world". They didn't plan or go too far ahead with their imagination. Rather they lived off of the sunny days and enjoyed being a part of the city that is always alive.

Vatican City – located on 44 HEKTARY of land attracts the tourists and the faithful from all around the world with its scenario of beauty and dignity at the same time. The population totaling of 800 people does not make an impression and it is the architecture, art and tradition that we admire.

It was not the first time for Mark and Andrzej that they followed the Vatican pathways. But each visit brought some new observations. They were happy to visit the place whenever possible.

Mark was trying to get through the solid crowd in order to get as close as possible to a tiny route through which the pope mobile was about to pass. He was indeed right up front. "What a shame Andrzej isn't here", he thought while far away he already coud see the car in which the Pope stood. "Will I be able to touch his hand?"

The car was slowly approaching and the Pope greeted everyone with a smile. A man in dark glasses dressed in a suit was passing first. He walked by Mark who thought, "It's the security service", and tried to reach as far from the fence as possible. He reached out with his hand and felt a touch'

- My name is Mark! – he yelled and in response heard from the Pope,
- God be with you, my son.

Mark wanted to say something else but a security guard clearly let him know he should get back deeper behind the barrier. But Mark was satisfied thinking happily: "I did it. I think he heard my name."

Andrzej meanwhile was getting to know the newcomers from the old country. All sat down at the steps of the basilica, waved the Polish flags and signs "Solidarity". The Pope has changed our lives. He proved that with self-determination, hard work and faith in ones strength we can do so much. He was the first Pole in decades to shine in the international arena and enjoyed incredible popularity. He speaks for millions of the faithful who together create the strongest religion of the world. Yet, looking at his life one can feel that he is one of us. So, thos visits to Vatican are not just opportunities to meet the Lord. They show also that no matter whom we are or where, we all belong to one mother whose name is Poland.

After the trip to Vatican two brothers were heading back to the hotel. Mark bragged how he tricked the security and manage to shake the Pope's hand. Andrzej reported on conversations he had with other Poles. They stopped by the Termini station. They liked it here – typical station traffic, passengers running all over and small merchants with colorful magazines added to the rhythm of life during this Roman afternoon. The two sat down on a bench and looked through the newspapers.

- Look who's running! He must need some money – Andrzej pointed.
- Who is it?
- Jasiek.
- Finally, I found you – Jasio said catching a breath – I was looking for you everywhere. I got some news.
- What is it?
- You don't know yet? We're leaving to the States. I'm flying with you. We're going to Detroit!
- When? – Andrzej asked.

- The day after tomorrow, on June 26.

They were packing their things anxiously. They were not too talkative to each other. After months spent in Italy it turned out they didn't have too much to take with them. Mark was looking through photos of his children and wife and placed them carefully in a bag. Andrzej took care of the dictionary and English language course book.

- We each have one luggage and 20 bucks in a pocket. - Andrzej said.
- That's it? Where is the rest?
- Girls are expensive – Andrzej tried to find an excuse.
- I know but we have less now then when we came to Italy. You ad your girls, bro, will get us gone bankrupt one day.
- Well, brother, you have bigger problem than I do. You try to plan everything ahead all the time. You even don't know what's around the corner but you always fear the worse. Use each day. Be happy every morning you wake up that you can live through another day. This is how I do it and life is much easier this way.

Mark didn't answer but inside he knew Andrzej had a point. He gave him a tap on the shoulder, grabbed his bag and left.

The airport in Rome hasn't changed a bit. The boys found the customs easily and it wasn't until they saw Boeing 747 when their imagination started to kick in. Great America, land of skyscrapers and large planes – it felt good when asked by some Italians where were they going, they could answer "New York". On the board they saw some Indian, the Chinese, the Vietnamese, black and whit Americans, the Arabs and Russians – some were coming back home while others were about to create one for themselves.

A pleasant flight attendant greeted everyone on behalf of the Alitalia airlines. After short introduction she asked to fasten the seatbelts. Two brothers were sitting in anxiety. Moments before the take off were like a nightmare. They felt like characters of a story, which was about to end, but it was the happy end that was still missing. The plane started to run. It sped up suddenly and took off the ground. Now all there was left was waiting.

CHAPTER IV

"In just a few moments we'll be landing in New York" - the flight attendant announced. Everyone on board started to get ready to leave. The luggage was checked and last drinks consumed. Anxiety was on the peak among the new immigrants as in just a short while they were about to see for the first time the "promised land". Mark was sitting next to a priest, who – as it turned out – was from Chicago. He told Mark about life in America. Andrzej and Jasio were sitting in the middle row and talked to the Vietnamese. The peaceful atmosphere was interrupted by a strange behavior of the plane. It was descending quickly. Everybody's hearts started to race. People were saying all around: "It is just a turbulence". In a moment the plane descended even more but this time its left side leaned downhill severely. Anxiety on passengers' faces kept rising. The machine descended again leaning to the side but it took longer than the previous time. Children were screaming. Remnants of cups and food were flying around the plane. It strengthened up but with double speed swayed again and started to descend rapidly. People started to scream fearfully. This time it was not just children but adults alike. "What's going on? We're falling!" The flight attendant, who a minute earlier tried to calm the crowd down, now disappeared behind the curtain. The plane was strengthening up and swaying to the side descending all the time. Some passengers who did not make it to refasten their seatbelts simply couldn't hold on to their seats. There was no doubt that something had happened, something that nobody could explain. Everything was pointing to the conclusion that the plane was falling down. Priest sitting next to Mark was praying heavily, but every time the plane would sway to the say he'd scream "Oh, my God". Childhood, school, college, marriage, children – all these pictures were going fast through Mark's mind. Andrzej was sitting peacefully but monitored the environment with huge anxiety at the same time watching for the luggage not to fall down on him. Everyone was certain that in a moment they were about to plunge with enormous strength into the depths of the ocean. People were holding each other's hands. Those who knew each other were hugging almost as to say "good bye". Silence. Even the children stopped crying. A sense of waiting was overwhelming. It was not, however, the kind of waiting that we know from every day life. It was waiting for death. Light STUKOT interrupted this silence and the plane started to descend somewhat gently. Everyone felt the Boeing's balance. The delicate noise of tires indicated that they landed. They were on the ground. Pale faces of passengers, whose clothes got messy from left over drinks and food, now smiled as if they were to say: "It's nice to be born again. They started to get up while the voice in the speakers announced: "Welcome to New York. We apologize for minor interruptions".

"Man to the right. Women and children to the left. Here are the I-94s to fill out", a man in uniform announced. The immigrants were walking around the waiting room trying to fill out their documents. Some sat on the floor, while others used back of their friends for that purpose. Two brothers were standing on the side with their documents ready. Their I-94s were already filled out thanks to the priest who sat with Mark. A man in uniform said:

- Come up to the window.

He spoke with typical American language, very different from the "English" that they were learning in Italy. They approached the window, showed their papers and signed a few more not having a clue what was it exactly that they were signing. After a few minutes they were free to leave. Andrzej pushed the door and left outside. Mark was right behind him.

- I will never again board a plane. That was crazy. I was sure that's it. What if we died? – Mark kept talking.
- That's history. I was scared myself, true. But after every night a new day comes up and after every storm there comes peace. Do you realize where you are? Forget about that plane and enjoy the States!

A young girl interrupted their conversation asking with full American accent.

- Excuse me; you guys are coming from Italy. Are you waiting for the plane to Detroit?

Two brothers stood without a word trying to understand what she said. After a minute Andrzej replied:

- Yes, we're going to Detroit.
- Well, this is an international airport. We need to move to a different terminal. Come on, I will show you and the gate from which you'll be leaving.

Mark thought: "Not another plane". The girl smiled and they started to walk. She tried to talk to them but it turned out that their English wasn't sufficient. After a while Mark said he wanted a beer, and so the girl showed him a mini bar saying: "Go, we have plenty of time". When Andrzej walked in to the place a pleasant barman asked him what he wanted. Andrzej happily ordered a beer; glad they understood what he asked for. He pulled out a twenty-dollar bill and placed it on the bar. Bartender gave him his change back and put the bottle in front. Andrzej counted his money and got very surprised: "Four bucks for a bottle of beer? That's crazy or he cheated me", he thought and walked out heading towards the girl.

- I'm not sure, but something around five dollars - she answered. And Andrzej thought, "She conspired with him". He said to his brother:

-   Listen, they charged me four bucks for a bottle of beer. That's robbery!
-   Give it a rest, brother. Even if they overcharged you two dollars or so, what are you going to do?
-   Two dollars? In Italy a beer costs 30 cents.

The girl understood what might be the problem and tried to explain to Andrzej that these, unfortunately, are the prices. As they kept walking along the airport Andrzej's good mood came back.

-   That's it- the girl said – your departure is in 20 minutes and there is your gate.

They said good-bye to her, shook her hand and the girl walked away.

-   What now? – Mark asked.
-   I guess we'll wait.
-   I know we'll wait but what next? We'll board the plane, land and what? Is someone going to pick us up? Do we have a place to stay?

The flight from New York to Detroit went without a major mark on two brothers. After the earlier adventure over the ocean, this could be considered and opportunity to finally get some rest. Once they landed it turned out that indeed there was a man waiting for them. He was Polish and took them from the airport to a house where they were to spend the first days in the United

States. It was a modest, one story house with a small garden in the back, and had aluminum siding. Inside of it looked like a museum; the doorknobs must have been from previous century, dinning set probably remembered time of great recession and bed and materace were brought bythe early pilgrims. The owner of this house, commonly known as „Pani Jadzia", welcomed them with a smile. She was a woman of average height, slightly leaned forward and was about 80 years old. She projected herself as quite an operative woman having lived in the United States for 50 years.

After the death of her husband the maintenance of the entire house rested on her shoulders. This is why she rented rooms to the new immigrants. She spoke good Polish but every once in a while she'd throw an English word to a Polish sentence. After the welcome she treated the guests with a glass of beer of which taste by no means resembled that of the European one. Afterward the time came for "pani Jadzia" to discuss the rules and regulations by which her kingdom operates.

- You can take a piss whenever you want but only the last one flushes – water is expensive and one has to use it wisely. The telephone is locked and if you need to use one you have to go to a pay phone. You can use the teapot but the rest of the pots and

155

pans are mine so if you want to cook
you have to go buy your own. No
smoking, only on the street. I also
don't want to see any strangers here
in the house. If you have some guests
let them wait on the street or in the
back yard. If you want to wash your
clothes, there is a Laundromat open
for the public not far away from the
house. This washer is mine and I
don't want you to use it. Also don't
park your car in front of my garage.
-   Can we breathe? – Andrzej asked.
    Pani Jadzia stopped and looked at him
    indifferently.
-   Yes, you can.
The afternoon with the lady of the house
ended. Everybody went to the back yard
relieved and commented on nonsense of the
rules and regulations they just heard.
Andrzej finally said:
-   Let's go to town to see America.
-   Don't we have to ask pani Jadzia for
    permission? – Leszek, one of the
    roommates, jokingly asked. The rest
    laughed and they all headed towards
    the street.
The overall impression of little houses –
wooden and brick – was depressing. Poorly
done store displays shined with lack of sense
of style and creativity. No neons or colorful
billboards added to the overall sad scenario.
Cars with rusty fenders and broken glasses
were passing by the street with no people.
Just seldom some random human ffigure
walked here or there. From each major street

156

several small ones were coming out and those were the little but long streets with houses on them. The rows of small wodden houses one very close to the next, with sharp peaks of roofing on top of them seemed to have no end. Small balconies with low railings – apparently as decorartion – were not helping the looks. Everything was surrounded by darkness. The newcomers were walking down and not saying anything just looked around. There was one conclusion to it and that is the only thing that the streets differed by were their names. Finally Mark broke the silence.

- What is it? Do you see what I see? It's like soviet labor camp, or something. Where are the hundred story buildings? Where the millions of people? Where the billboards and the beautiful cars? They must have brought us to a movie set where they shoot motion picture from the previous century. This is so lame I can hardly speak.

The others shared in his disbelief. They didn't think that what they would see in America was so far away from their expectations. Even Andrzej, who usually was the most optimistic guy, this time lost his cheer. It was the first time in his life, that he felt so disappointed. He couldn't believe that this was the end. But he also knew that this was just the beginning. But how long will it take to get to the point called "success"? How much of the sacrifice and ups and downs will it take to get satisfied? Will it ever happen?

It is located in the middle of Detroit, has its own administration, its own mayor, police and fire station. Some 20 thousand people proudly announce that they live in the city of Hamtramck. It is a typical, blue collar, American town where many Poles arrived during the course of the years. They were coming to work in big auto plants, which surrounded Hamtramck. And with time it got a reputation of being the "Polish town". Its stores and restaurants, clubs and statue of John Paul II suggested a close connection between its inhabitants and the history and tradition they brought with them. Three large churches are there to fulfill their religious needs and the crown of the Polish domination in town happens during the annual festival in town, during which one can watch and hear Polish songs dances and taste some excellent Polish food. Polish language is heard everywhere and some don't even bother learning English. They work for and with other Polish people, buy their groceries in Polish stores and do the banking in the Polish bank. Once more there is a testimony that Poland is where the Poles are. But Hamtramck is known not just for the ethnic peculiarity – the amount of bars per capita is so high that the city became number one in the country when it comes to this aspect. Is it something to be proud of? Hard to tell but one think is certain – the bar business is flourishing.

After the first week two brothers stopped paying attention to the looks of the city. They saw it all by now. The next step was Detroit with its downtown. They didn't have a car, which – as it turned out – is a necessity to survive there, as it is the only means of transportation to use. Yes, there are bus lines but nobody really knew where do they go or from where they started. Luckily the boys met Mrs. Tarnowski. Mrs. Adela – that was her ffirst name – worked for the Tolstoy Foundation dealing with immigrants arriving to the states. She spoke good Polish and what is most important was a very good-natured woman always ready to help the newcomers. It was thank to her efforts that she was able to get the boys some financial help from the government. That enabled them to pay "pani Jadzia" and buy some food. She also assisted Mark in writing up a letter to both Polish and American authorities with the purpose of getting Mark's family over to America. Together they also filled out the paperwork necessary for Andrzej and Mark to obtain their permanent residence in the United States, the so-called "green card".

- Congratulations. – Adela. – Now you are fully lawful Americans.

The boys looked at each other smiling and Mark said:

- Thanks for everything, Adela, you've helped us a great deal and we are grateful for that. I just have one question.
- What is it?

159

- When will I be able to see my wife and children?
- I can't give you a precise answer. But the worse case scenario is two years.

Mark looked at her with a smile:

- The worse case scenario? – he asked and Adela nodded affirmative.
  Andrzej interrupted:
- And the best case scenario is they will be here tomorrow. Mark why ask stupid questions? She can't know when everything will be finalized besides we have to get back on our feet ourselves. Can you imagine what it would be like if Aneta and the kids came and you'd have to live at pani Jadzia's?

Everybody laughed at this. Andrzej said:

- Adela, I also have a question.
- Go ahead.
- Where are we? I mean what part of Michigan, and what part of Detroit? Where are the famous great lakes? We still don't have a map and walk around town like a fly in a jar.
- Everything is simple. All you have to know is where is north. In the whole country freeways and expressways numbered with odd numbers go from north to south. Like I-75; you can take it from Michigan all the way to Florida. The ones numbered with even numbers go from East to West. Well, in our metro Detroit the situation is similar; starting in the southern part towards north instead of

160

giving streets names, they numbered them by miles. It starts in downtown Detroit, right at the border with Canada.
- So what mile road are we at right now?
- In proximity, Hamtramck is between the fourth and the sixth mile.
- Hold on, you said the mile roads go from south towards north.
- That's right.
- But then you said that mile roads go from Detroit, from the south where there's border with Canada. Since when do you go south in order to get to Canada?
- Good observation. Michigan is probably the only state where can reacho Canada going south.
- How many miles north does Detroit spread to?
- You have to understand that metro Detroit is not the same as the city of Detroit itself. The city ends on 8 mile road, but the metro area goes all the way to 40th mile. Between the 8th and the 40th mile there are various cities and towns located. They are all independent with own administration, courthouses, police and fire stations. But they all belong to what is called metro.
- Ok, and so where are the lakes? – Mark asked.
- You'll have more than one chance to admire them. Detroit is right by Lake

St. Clair, which connects with the
great lake Huron. Now Huron goes
north all the way to lake Michigan.
But you can check all this on the map;
I really must go now.
They said goodbye and Adela went to her car
and left.

- Cool girl – Andrzej said.
- You say "cool girl meaning as friend
  or as a woman?

Mark just shook his head in despair:

- You only think about one thing, don't
  you?
- Well, and what did you think; oh I'm
  in America so I can' t even look at a
  woman anymore? It's for the women
  that we came here in the first place.
  Why make money, to keep in a bank?
  Money is not the most important
  thing but it is the means, which leads
  us to women.
- Please, enough. Right now them
  most important thing is job – we have
  to find one and start making some
  money.
- Job, my brother, is not the most
  pleasant word.
- And what difference does it make?
- Maybe none, but should someone ask
  me what do I do? I'd rather say: "I'm
  fishing the money" rather then I work
  for it.

Mark busted out laughing.

- All right, starting tomorrow we're
  looking for the pond.

The great America closed up within the circle
of one small town. The boys tried to find
some work but it was impossible without
having a car. Most jobs offered were in the
service industry – restaurants, stores, gas
stations. Hamtramck did not have much of
the manufacturing industry, besides two
factories making pierogis and kielbasa.
There was also a General Motors plant where
they tried to get hired in but unsuccessfully.
It was a small town with small amount of
jobs for small money. This would be the best
assessment of Hamtramck's job market but
the boys did not give up. They did whatever
they had to do; cleaned offices, paint
apartments, fix rooftops. One day Mark
found out that there was an opening in a
bakery.
A short, heavyset guy with gray hair stood in
front of the shop smoking cigar.
- Good morning – Mark started.
- Good morning.
- Are you Ray – the owner?
- That would be me.
- I'd like to work here.
- And what is it that you can do?
Mark, taken by the question, paused for a
minute thinking "What can I do? Well,
besides reading books and passing exams
I've never really done anything like this in
my life. What did I come here for?" But he
asked the owner:
- What is it that needs to be done?
The owner looked at Mark and said:

-   That's what I thought; you can't do
    anything. But you look all right.
    You'll be cleaning.

Mark breathed relieved; "I have a job. That's
something".

-   What exactly do you want me to
    clean?
-   Why don't you start with the sidewalk
    in front of the bakery. The do the
    shop and the back of the bakery at the
    end.
-   And once I'm done? – Mark asked.
    Ray looked at him somewhat strange:
-   Once you're done, you'll start all over
    again.

Mark wanted to say something but paused for
a moment. Finally he asked:

-   How much per hour will you pay me?

Ray let the smoke out of his mouth. He
opened it widely. At this moment Mark
heard a loud rumbling, looked around in case
there was a car with broken exhaust passing
by. Quickly he looked back at Ray and
thought "what a belch". Ray smiling looked
at Mark and asked

-   Did I scare you?
-   Not really, but I do admit that I've
    never heard anyone belch so loud
    before.
-   You'll get three buck an hour.
-   When can I start?
-   What you mean? Now, right away.
    Go inside, the girls will hook you up
    with brooms and dustpans.

Mark headed towards the entrance of the
store. His thoughts: "I have a job. After 16

164

years of schooling I'll be cleaning p a
sidewalk, store and the bakery. And after a
few years, once I get the necessary
experience, I'll still be cleaning a sidewalk,
store and bakery". He kept on walking but
deep inside he was happy.

On the East side of town, by one of the major
streets there was a Polish club. Large, good-
looking, brick building had a dance floor, bar
and a few small rooms used according to the
occasion. The main occupation of the
patrons was drinking beer - eventually
stronger drinks – smoking cigarettes, playing
cards and pool. Just from time to time the
Polish boy scouts organization had its
meetings there, or there was a concert of
some guest artist, or a party. Others than that
the place lived off its monotony. I is
amazing how quickly most of the men
succumb to the bar customs, giving up
thousands of other ways to spend free time.
The same conversations on the same subjects,
political disappointments, spurs of historic
pride mingled with local gossip column.
Andrzej leaned over the pool table taking his
time to hit the white ball precisely. It rolled
on the green just to hit another ball.
- I missed again – he said.
- Don't worry. Practice makes perfect
  – cheered Heniu – Andrzej's bar-
  buddy.
- Fine, but how long will the practice
  take?
- You wont even know when a day will
  come you'll get every shot.

165

- Ok, you won. I'm buying.

They sat at the bar. Andrzej ordered another beer as they kept quiet.

- Do you work? – Andrzej asked.
- Yeah.
- Can you get me into wherever it is that you work?
- That's funny. You don't even know what I do but you know you want to work there. Tell me better hat is it that you can do? I'll tell you if there is a chance for you there.
- I can do pretty much anything. How about that?
- Well, I work dismantling stuff. It's a hard job. We walk around production halls trying to retrieve whatever from old equipment; copper, lead, stainless steel, etc. We use heavy saws for that. Once we chop whatever, we need we load it on trucks. And it's like this over and over again. If you want I can take you tomorrow. You'll talk to my boss tomorrow; see if he'd hire you. Then maybe we could work together. Deal?
- Why did you ask me what I can do? From what you're telling me the only thing one needs to know how to do in this job.
- What is it?
- How to walk – Andrzej answered laughing – but enough joking. Thanks a lot. I'll go tomorrow and I hope it'll work out. Come on now, let's shot another game.

The immigrant life of the two brothers started to go according to a routine. Andrzej did get the job. It wasn't – as he originally thought – as easy, though. The motor saw got heavier and heavier every day. The noise of cutting steel gave him headaches and the stench of fumes took away his appetite. Mark still was taking care of the sidewalk, store and bakery, which were all getting dirty just as quickly as they were getting clean. The monotony entered their lives and caused them to forget sometimes that they were in America. Every day was just like the previous one, blisters on hands, fatigue – they covered up the America's glamour.

Andrzej walked to the room

- Hi.
- What's new at work? – Mark replied.
- Like there's ever anything new. We cut, we load and count days to the weekend. I'm tired with this shit.
- Come on, I'll show you something that will cheer you up.

They walked outside. Mark grabbed Andrzej by the hand as they approached a blue car.

- Do you like it?
- Not bad. Do you thin about buying?
- I already have.

Andrzej looked at him in disbelief.

- And you didn't even ask me about it?
- I wanted to surprise you.
- Well, you did.
- It's Potiac Sunbird; 2.5, V-4, automatic, stereo inside, 40K mileage.
- Good, good. How much did you pay?

167

- $1600.
- Very good – Andrzej was pleased with the deal his brother made.
- So, going for a ride?
- Sure thing. Finally we'll get to see Detroit.

They sat in the car and smiled; once again they felt released from the daily worries. The car started with squeaking tires. They reached Woodward Ave., which is one of Detroit's main streets. From 8 Mile they headed south to get to downtown. Loud music and conversations about the future put them in excellent mood. As they kept driving the look of the city grabbed their attention more and more. Dirty street, old, scrapped buildings, stores with crates in the windows started to scare them. Even the prostitutes walking down the streets looked totally unattractive.

- Look, Mark. These are all black people.
- I can see. Maybe it's a black neighborhood and it will be different in a while.

They kept on driving but the difference they expected did not occur. Andrzej said:

- Gee, nothing changes. This isn't a city. This is ghetto.
- Where are all the white people? – Mark wondered.

Andrzej didn't say anything because he simply didn't know. They drove in to downtown and the skyscrapers grabbed their attention. The tallest of them was the Renaissance Center, headquarters of the

General Motors Corporation. It looked powerful with its glass structure. Then spread nicely by the river there were Joe Louis arena, and exhibition center, "Cobo". On the opposite side of the river gently waived flags with the maple leave on them, invitig everyone to come to Canada, to the city of Windsor connected with Detroit by The Ambassador bridge and a tunnel running under the waters of Detroit river. Two brothers observed the cars coming to and out of the tunnel. The behavior of the border security officers surprised them as they hardly ever even looked in trunks of the cars.

- Once we get our green cards, we'll go to Canada – Andrzej said.
- Definitely. We have to see Michal. I'm sure he's already there. I wander if Canada differs from U.S. at all.
- Either way, it'll be still nice to go. You know what, though? Those skyscrapers, the tunnel and the bridge – now that is somewhat America. I'm glad we came here to downtown as I started to doubt we would ever get to see the America.
- I like downtown, but I don't understand why the rest of the city is so neglected. This is the richest country in the world. I can't believe they don't have the money to work on those buildings a bit – Mark was truly in disbelief, but Andrzej tried to reason:
- You still live in some dreamland. Look, the great buildings here, the

169

glass ones etc., they belong to GM and to the banks, all of which have the money. The little dirty ones probably belong to those who don't have it and who can't restore them, and why they don't have the money? Because they're lazy and don't want to work. Is this simple or what?

- Seems like it, but what if it turns out that those people actually do work very hard but can't afford much anyway?

- You're just looking for a way to wear me out. Stop thinking "what if" so much and start being happy that you're in America.

- Ok now. Let's get back to Hamtramck. We'll grab a beer at the Polish club.

- Now you're talking like Polskowicz – Andrzej summed it up.

At the bar a man was telling a story:

- So I'm driving like a hundred an hour, or so. Nice, straight freeway, beautiful weather, my "caddie" drives smooth. Then all of the sudden I look and there's a cop behind me. Turns his lights on and pulls me over. "What is it about?" – I asked and he goes: "You were driving to fast". I'm like: "What you mean? The speed limit is 94 per hour". The cop looks at me as if I'm an idiot so I show him a sign, where it says "94". He busts out laughing and tells me that this was a number of the freeway I was on, not

170

the speed limit post. I got speechless.
He said something else but didn't
give me a ticket, just kept laughing
like crazy.
- Are you for real? – Andrzej asked
    sipping on the beer. He couldn't
    believe the story.
- I swear.
Andrzej kept looking at the guy;
- How long have you lived in America?
- It will be a year.
- You really should have got the ticket,
    not for speed but for being stupid.
The guy got up from the table, grabbed the
empty bottle and aimed at Andrzej. He
knocked the bottle out of his hand and got the
guy by his shirt al the way to the ground.
The guy fell but quickly picked himself up
and rushed towards Andrzej again. This time
Andrzej grabbed his hand, twisted it to the
back and escorted the guy to the door.
- I will see you again – the guy
    threatened on the way out.
- Come back when you're not so dumb
    anymore.
Andrzej came back and sat at the bar next to
Mark.
- We have to move – he said to Mark.
- Why?
- I don't want to end up like that moron
    who can't tell the difference between
    signs. Pointless job, bar and sleeping
    – this lifestyle leads to that. There's
    got to be a different, better and
    happier way of life.
Andrzej asked the barmaid:

- Can I have two shots?
- I don't want any – Mark protested.
- Come on, we have to drink to the car.
The barmaid passed them the vodka, which
the brothers clinked and drank.
- Give us one more! – Andrzej asked
  again. This time Mark was not
  protesting. Andrzej asked him:
- When is Aneta supposed to come?
- From the last letter I got from her, it
  seems like she will come on six
  months or so.
- Well, we have six months to find a
  place in this country. If we don't
  check it out for ourselves, we'll never
  know if Detroit is indeed the place.
- What's on your mind? – Mark asked
  anxiously.
- We're leaving, now, right now!
  Screw the job both yours and mine.
  There has to be a place where they
  pay better, where the houses are
  colorful and stores have nice displays.
  In worse case at least where the
  hookers are better looking.
They both laughed and Andrzej yelled;
- One more round for us!
- Where would you want to go? – Mark
  asked.
- California – Andrzej shouted without
  thinking much.

The car kept going smooth and Andrzej
looked up the starry sky every now and then.
Mark slept on the passenger seat. They
already went through Ohio and Indiana.

Now they were in Illinois, just minutes away from Chicago. Andrzej tried to wake his brother up. He opened his eyes and looked around.

- Where are we?
- We'll be in Chicago in a moment.
- Nice going. I really had to get pretty tanked to agree to this trip. Are you serious about going to California?
- You bet I am. Look, we're in Chicago now. Tomorrow we'll be in Denver and the day after in Los Angeles.
- How much money do we have?
- Three hundred.
- That's it? Where's the rest?
- In the bank in Detroit. – Andrzej answered patiently – We left at 2 a.m. How was I supposed to withdraw anything?

Mark had to agree, but asked:

- Gas, hotels, food – how do you Imagine all this?
- Don't panic. Gas isn't that expensive. We'll e fine to get to L.A. money wise. We'll skip the hotels. We can sleep in the car and we'll eat whatever we can afford.
- You're really crazy. Come on, turn around and let's go back to Detroit.
- Chill out and think: a trip like this may not ever happen to you again. Besides, maybe it is better out west. Today you have a chance to go to California for three hundred bucks. If you go back and count how much

173

would it cost you to get to L.A. you'll
probably end up with two or three
grand. And what? You'll be cleaning
that bakery for the rest of your life
and never even put that money away.
Mark listened to it somewhat upset. He
wanted to say something but meanwhile they
drove in to the city and the traffic got
heavier. The six-lane freeway was full of
life. The cars sped one after another. On the
left the people mover filled with passengers
headed deeper into the city. Far ahead,
almost like a mountaintop, there was
downtown revealing itself.
-    Wow, beautiful – Mark said.
-    See, told you. This is America. And
      what if it's just the beginning.
The drove in to the heart of the city. Even
though it was early morning the traffic on the
streets was surprisingly heavy. People going
from place to place, from one building to
another. Cars drove slower and there was
virtually no parking place empty. The
brothers passed by the Sears Tower, which
was the tallest building in the world, and
headed towards the lake.
-    Mark look, it's Baltic.
Mark looked ahead of him and far away he
saw the never-ending surface of water.
Expensive yachts kept rocking on the water.
Some were of the size of a house. In the
distance one could spot cargo ships, which
looked like oceanic carriers.
-    This is amazing – Mark wasn't trying
      to hide his admiration - This city
      lives, I feel like I'm in Rome.

174

- So, was I right or what?
- You were – Mark answered with humbleness.
- Chicago is just the beginning – Andrzej kept on talking – I wander what else is there for us to see on the way.
- Andrzej, let's go to Polish town. To be in Chicago and not to visit the countrymen, now that would be a sin.
- That is a good idea. Plus we could hook up with "manager", our buddy from the camp, remember?
- Do you have his number?
- I sure do. And guess what? – I also have the number to Jola and Lukasz in L.A.
- You know, you're not as dumb as you look – Mark joked and they both laughed.
- Finally there will be an opportunity to put to use the old camp contacts.

The Polish town in Chicago, called "Jackowo", looks fairly similar to other Polish neighborhoods throughout the States: Polish stores, restaurants, travel agencies, doctors' offices and bookstores. All of this fully satisfies the needs of immigrants. The cultural life, however, was a lot more intense here then elsewhere. Various concerts, promotions, exhibitions sponsored by Polish radio stations made the Polish language, culture and tradition an integral part of Chicago every day life. Hence the reason

175

why some call Chicago the capitol of Polish immigrants in America.

The brothers met their camp buddy, "manager" and shared their impressions on American culture, architecture, job situation and wages. There was no doubt that Chicago beat Detroit in each aspect.
- Like a capitol, huh?
- Why these people come in to this bar and leave almost right away? – Mark asked the "Manager".
- They only come to use the restroom.
- They don't order anything from the bar?
- That what it seems like.

Andrzej was listening to this and added:
- We'll clear out the situation in a moment.
- Miss, could you come up here to us for a moment? – he asked the barmaid. As she approached he ordered:
- I'd like three Polish beers.
- Not a problem.

As she was about to walk away, he asked:
- Who allows these people to walk in to a bar and use restroom without even paying?
- This you would have to discuss with Mr. Mecio.
- With Mietek?
- So, you know him?
- Of course – Andrzej was lying – not only do I know him but we do business together.

Mark and "Manager" were listening to this conversation not knowing where it was going.

- Oh God, so you are the new owner?

Andrzej kept silent for a minute to gather his thoughts and put all facts together.

- You got it. And I thought that Mietek didn't tell anybody.
- The barmaid stood somewhat embarrassed and finally said:
- Mr. Miecio told me he had sold the bar but he didn't want to say to whom.
- That's no biggie. But I was wondering why people come in to use the restroom and don't spend any money?
- This is a very good point and I talked with Mr. Miecio about it many times.
- Well, how would you solve this situation?

The barmaid looked at him with gratitude and proudly answered:

- Finally someone asked me for an opinion. I would solve it very simply – there should be a sign posted by the restroom, which says if someone who is not a patron wants to use a restroom, they should pay 20 cents.
- Very good – Andrzej answered and reached his hand out to her. She shok it and said:
- How should I address you?
- You can just call me by my name. I'm Andrzej.
- And I'm Renia.

- Very nice to meet you. Now could
  we have those beers?
- Oh, I completely forgot because of all
  this.

She walked away.

- What the hell are you doing? – Mark
  asked. - You want to get the cops and
  the owner o our back or what?
- It's not going to be that bad. –
  "Manager" answered for him – She
  really believes that he is the new
  owner.
- Let's better get this beer, finish up
  and go – Mark said.

Renia came back to the table. She put the
beers in front of Andrzej along with a white
envelope.

- What is it? – Andrzej asked.
- It's today's sales – She answered and
  explained – Mr. Mieciu usually
  collects it around this time of the day.

Andrzej looked inside of it and saw carefully
placed bills. He sealed the envelope and
gave it back to Renia.

- Why don't you give it to Mietek. I'm
  really busy today and I won't have a
  chance to get to the bank.
- Whatever you like.

The boys drank their beers and left.
"Manager" said:

- You could have taken the money. It's
  not like you have a lot.
- But I'm not a thief. I just wanted to
  see if I really convinced her that I am
  the new owner. It worked and I'm
  glad. But have I taken the money,

you and Mark would also think that –
like it or not – I am a thief.

- Maybe you're right. I'm telling you –
with the bullshit that you can pull you
don't have to worry about getting
through life.

The boys walked up to the car and said
goodbye to the "Manager". Polish names
and signs on the street were slowly getting
smaller and less visible as they were driving
away. Finally they disappeared blended in
the Chicago reality. The car drove smooth on
the freeway and Mark turned the radio to the
station with some Chicago blues. Andrzej
was studying the map.

- Iowa, Nebraska and Colorado.
- What's after? – Mark asked.
- Then there's Utah, Nevada, Arizona
and California. I'm gonna sleep now,
but wake me up in like ten ours and
I'll drive.

Iowa was somewhat of a surprise to Mark.
The colorful farms were dragging for miles.
He passed the Mississippi river and expected
some variety in the scenario. With mixed
feelings of disappointment and interest he
looked at cornfields. A million and half acres
of forests finally made hi realize why the
Indian name of the state; "ayutwa" means
"beautiful land". He reached the western part
of the state and noticed that plane fields
started to be elevated. It wasn't any dramatic
change but after hours of looking at planes
and fields only sometimes interrupted by
forests, the thirty and hundred meter tall hills
seemed like humongous mountains. "This is

the SPICHLERZ of America", he thought
and then saw a sign saying "Missouri River".

- Wake up! – he yelled at Andrzej –
  you slept through whole Iowa. We're
  entering Nebraska now, look!

Andrzej rubbed his eyes and looked around.

- Did they manage to cut down all trees
  here already, or what?
- You know, you're right. One can
  count them with one had.
- Well, maybe it just looks like that
  now. We'll see what's behind the
  hill.

But after the hill there was a small valley,
and after the valley there was another small
hill. The boys didn't realize that they were in
a land without trees, with occasional sand
hills. After a while they passed by a
gorgeous sunflower field and headed south,
towards Platte river.

- Did you know that Fred Astaire and
  Marlon Brando were from Nebraska?
  – Andrzej was quizzing his brother.
- I didn't know that. But now did you
  know that it was in Nebraska where in
  1982 the corporations were banned
  from buying companies? That's why
  the farmers have s much to show off
  here.
- Aaa, there is Mr. Zootechnician.
- Look! – Mark pointed with his hand
  to the tall stone-sand peak – This is
  the Chimney Rock, which for
  centuries allowed the travelers to
  realize the direction. Now we know

180

that we're going in the right direction
to Colorado.
- Like we couldn't check it on the map.
- Feel like you're one of the pioneers
  who were going out west.
- You're right, I already feel like one
  and I feel hungry like a pioneer too.
Mark smiled somewhat mysteriously and
pulled up by a gas station.. Andrzej asked:
- So what are we getting to eat?
- Same as usual.
- Bread and farmer's cheese? That's
  too expensive. We have to change
  our menu.
- What do you mean? This is the
  minimum we can eat. My stomach
  has been bothering me for days now.
  I don't say anything nor complain but
  we have to eat something at least.
- Let's try bread and mustard today.
They disputed for a while and finally Andrzej
convinced Mark that they really have to save
as much as possible.
- You just never know what is going to
  happen along the way – he kept
  repeating. So the brothers
  compromised; they got mustard and
  eggs.
- Now, how are you going to cook
  these eggs? – Andrzej asked.
- Don't worry about that. We'll ask at
  the nearest house and I'm sure they
  won't refuse us some boiling water.
Mark spotted a farm not far away, turned and
came up front. A woman came out on the
stairs and the brothers greeted her politely

and asked if they could cook some eggs. She smiled and said there would not be a problem. They waited outside while the woman disappeared behind the door.

- Put your hands up! – a man said to them coming toward them from the side.
- Who sent you here?

Andrzej wanted to turn and explain the situation. Quickly he felt the cold of the gun up on his shoulder.

- Don't move or I'll shoot.
- Nobody sent us. We're on the way to California and jus wanted to cook some eggs.
- For as long as I live, I've never heard a better story.

From far away they heard noise of a car. Andrzej spotted with his eye that it was a police car. A cop came up to them and checked what they had. Then he searched their car.

- You're lucky you don't have any weapons. You'd be in my jail by now.

The brothers looked at him somewhat surprised.

- Look, we're just here on the way to…
- Yeah, on the way to California, right? I have 180 bucks but you're on the way to California. You can tell this bullshit in a kindergarten but not to me.
- Our friends have the rest of our money and they wait for us in Denver. – Andrzej started explaining

confidently – We made a bet that we can convince a farm owner to cook those eggs for us. So we came up here and our friends – as it turned out – left and kept driving.

The cop listened to this story and whispered something to the farmer.

- Ok, there is 15 minutes to the Colorado border. Get in your car and I'll follow you. Once you enter Colorado go straight ahead to Denver, and I better don't see you in my area anymore.

Andrzej drove the car calmly just glancing at the mirror occasionally to check if the overly inspired cop still follows him. When he saw the sign: "Welcome to Colorado" he sped up:

- Kiss my ass you stupid cop – he yelled as they crossed the state border.
- I never thought that we'd be treated like bandits in America – Mark said.
- Well, what were you thinking, that you're n Poland where everybody is Polish? This is the place where all outcasts from the entire world come and you never know whom you can meet?
- I understand what you're saying, Mark, but that cop didn't want to help us – period. More so, it seemed as if he were mad for not being able to put us in jail.
- That's how life is – people try to see everything bad and whatever the good stuff, goes forgotten fast.

- You're right. But that story about
  our buddies waiting for us in Denver
  – I have to give you credit; it was
  great. Slowly I'm starting to buy into
  your lies.

The brothers quickly forgot about the
unpleasant episode in Nebraska. The hilly
scenery of the environment grabbed their
attention now. They were going through the
American Switzerland. An average height of
the hills in Colorado is around 2 kilometers.
Colorado means red, and it refers to the water
in the Colorado river. The black canyon that
goes for over a 100 kilometers, takes the
breath away from even the most demanding
tourists. Luxury houses blended in the
mountain scenario overlook the freeway like
the eagles' nests.

- I wonder where are all the gold and
  silver mines – Mark said.
- Once we pass Denver we should see
  them.
- I heard that near Aspen they once
  found a gold rock they weighed
  around 900 grams.
- What is the highest peak? – Mark
  kept asking.
- Probably Mt. Elbert; five thousand
  meters – Andrzej replied.
- When did you have time to read about
  all this?

Andrzej wanted to answer but couldn't, as all
of the sudden from underneath the front hood
streams of smoke started to pour.

- Shit! Something's wrong with the
  radiator – Mark yelled.

184

- Like that's what we need now.

The boys stopped on the shoulder to check what happened. Indeed, a rubber hose that connected the radiator broke, which wasn't too much of a big deal but in their circumstances it became a serious issue. So they stood on the side of the road trying to stop the passing cars.

- This is not Poland – Mark said – Nobody's gonna give you a ride anywhere.
- Don't jinx it. Just keep on trying. Someone will stop finally.

They were like that to the sunset and the hope for any sort of help was getting weaker with every minute.

- Look! - Mark shouted pointing at the upcoming car – He's pulling over!

Mark was right. A driver with a smile stopped. He grabbed his towing line and towed their car to Denver. In a small garage on the outskirts of the city, and old mechanic took a look at the broken part. Without a question he started to work on it. After half an hour the car was ready to go. The brothers praised the "boss" for his quick and professional intervention but their joy ended once they heard how much they had to pay.

- A hundred dollars? – Andrzej yelled – For a hundred bucks I could replace the engine! This is a piece of rubber! – he kept screaming to the "boss".

The owner of the shop tried to explain them that he worked after hours and was fast, indeed. Seeing, however, that he was not going to convince Andrzej, he simply said:

185

- The work is done. Either you pay or I'm calling the cops. "There come the cops again" – Mark thought. Andrzej saw the unhappy face of his brother, waited a moment and finally made an offer:
- Look, we don't have that much money, but we can trade.
- What trade? – the mechanic asked.
- I'll give you two brand new front tires, while you give me two old ones. I'm sure that's worthy of a hundred bucks.

The mechanic thought a moment and finally said "ok". He switched the tires quickly and the brothers were momentarily back on the road.

- Next time you'll trade my car for a bicycle – Mark said.
- Did we have any other choice?

They were getting tired and it showed. Without enough of sleep, hungry they gave up admiring the beauty of nature. Utah made no impression on them besides the twenty kilometer long piece of freeway, where world speeding records are established.

Grand Canyon in Arizona did, however, "wake them up". They regretted very much that they could not afford a hotel. They wish they could admire the view that shocked them with its beauty and might.

- This is where Apaches lived – Andrzej started – This is where their territory was until Geronimo led them out to Florida.

186

- That's sad that they had to leave their land fearing the white people – Mark said.
- The white were stronger, better organized and armored.
- Yeah, but doesn't it seem to you like the Indians are the only ones who fit this land? Our cars, suits, ironed shirts and women with pretty make up have nothing to do with this colorful but rough scene.
- I see, you're back to your sentimental approach to life – Andrzej replied.
- This is not sentimental, Andrzej - Mark said – Look, we've been traveling for four days, seen great deal of the world, and besides the nature nothing really makes one state different than the other. The hotels are alike and even sometime have the same names. The same thing with the gas station – same names and decorations. The freeways differ by numbers only, and finally the restaurants and food are the same, as well.
- In other words, what you really want to say is that you don't really like it that much in the States, right?
- No, I didn't mean that, just that something is missing.

They entered the state of Nevada. The first sign they saw reminded the drivers to fill up their gas tanks and get a good supply of water as the next service station will be no sooner

187

than some 200 kilometers away. As opposed to other states, Nevada in 80% belongs to the government. Dry and worse climate, lack of crop fields and deficit of water are behind the fact that only small gold mines remind that there are still people present. Hence, even though the state is of the size of Poland, some two million people only inhabit it, half of which live in Las Vegas.

- Why, for God's sake, did you have to play in the casino? – Mark asked.
- To be in Vegas and not to play in a casino is like coming in to church and not make a sign of the cross.
- Oh really? And how much money do we have left?

Andrzej kept quiet.

- Well, go ahead – tell me how much for real do we have left?
- We have a full tank of gas and twenty-five dollars.

Mark was quiet; he was mad. On the other hand he knew he should say what he said. In fact, he himself was somewhat happy walking into the casino and playing a bit. Overall this was Vegas.

More than 300 thousand square kilometers and thirty million people – if California were an independent country it would be the sixth industrial power. Twenty three million cars every day travels through different areas of the state. The brothers drove in to Los Angeles and the atmosphere of this atmosphere absorbed them almost instantly.

Andrzej was studying the map. He wanted
very much to find the street where their
friends from Latina lived. They were in the
States a little shorter than Mark and Andrzej ,
but – as Andrzej used to say – they ended up
living in paradise.

- There it is! I found it! – Andrzej
  screamed.
- Well, then tell me where to go
  because if we miss the exit it'll take
  us forever to go back.
- The very next exit – Pico Boulevard.
  – Andrzej instructed and they soon
  took the exit.
- You know, they live in Hollywood –
  Andrzej continued talking.
- You're kidding.
- Seriously.

The brothers soon saw the famous sign on the
hill afar: "Hollywood". But as they kept
driving towards the capitol of the film
industry their expectations turned into a big
disappointment.

- Tell me it doesn't remind you of
  Detroit – Andrzej started.
- You're right.
- We drove thousands of miles just to
  see what we've already seen.

They found the address where their friends
lived. Mark was waiting in the car and
Andrzej went to say "hallo". After a moment
he was back and sat n the car unhappy.

- They no longer live there. They
  moved a week ago.

- Oh, great. Now we're really screwed. Don't the new people know their current address?
- No, by the door there is a telephone. I tried to call but it's broken.
- So what do we do now?
- I don't know yet. Let's drive the main street. We'll sit somewhere and try to figure something out.

They went to Hollywood Boulevard, parked their car and sat on the curb.

- We have twenty bucks and some gas. – Andrzej said.
- I know, I know. We'll sleep in the car and in the morning but the paper. We'll look for some jobs and somehow it will work out.
- You know what?
- Yeah?
- I've never felt so humiliated as I do now. I understand those people without homes, without jobs, who sleep on the streets and in their faces there is just no expression. They accepted their fate. This is their life. They surely have their problems and worries. Sometimes they may be even happy. But all in all – nobody pays attention to them. They are like a piece of the general city existence. Even if sometimes a guy in a suit will give them some change in changes nothing for the guy in a suit also accepts his fate and rarely smiles. In fact I feel sorry for both of them.

- Don't get emotional here over the homeless people – Andrzej said – the rich and the poor have always been around. This is how this world works – some works for others. What – would you like to introduce socialism to America, or what?
- No, but our situation make me realize how little do we mean in this greatcity.
- Maybe, but we mean that much as not to dye of starvation.

They continued their discussion sitting on the curb and finally their own fate smiled at them as they heard the familiar voice.

- God, what are you guys doing here? – a girl asked coming up to them. They looked at her with surprise. First of all somebody spoke Polish, and second of all it was Jola – the very Jola they were looking for.
- This is the last thing I'd expect – Andrzej said with a smile – that I would see you again ever. Seeing you now here in Hollywood – now that is a miracle.
- I live close from here and take this street everyday. You guys were lucky to pick this spot to sit down. Come on; let's go to my place. Tell me what brought you from the cold Michigan to paradise?
- Paradise? – Mark said ironically. Andrzej gave him a look that prevented him from additional comments. Andrzej started to tell her

191

the story as thy walked down Hollywood Boulevard. He told her how abruptly they decided to leave Detroit. He also mentioned the episode on the plane to New York and finally all three of them came back to good memories of Latina and Rome.

They didn't have a problem finding jobs. Of course those were not position matching their education; Mark painted houses, worked in gardens and poured concrete. Andrzej got a job welding in a small company, to which he lied what an experience welder from Poland he was. They weren't making much but they could afford to take time off on the outskirts of the city or going to the beach picnics. Spending time in waters of the Pacific and surfing classes filled most of their spare time. They quickly realized that the city of Los Angeles was divided into neighborhoods, of which looks were proportional to the earnings of their residents; the ones on the south eastern side were poor while the ones on north western part, with Beverly Hills, were very rich. The place where they stayed was in east Hollywood, but in spite of the nice name it was located in poor area of L.A. Sometimes coming back from somewhere on Saturday evening they wished they could do more than just watch the attractive clubs and restaurants. With time they got to know Sunset Boulevard better. You could call it Entertainment Street; good looking prostitutes, gays, clusters of punks and hippie people mingled with black and Latino gang members. Everything was blended I colorful signs of bars and inviting advertisings for sex-shops, giving it all a look of extraterrestrial civilization.

- How do you like the Sunset Boulevard? – Andrzej asked.
- It is colorful. I have not seen that crazy of the company in my life.
- This is California. People live one day at the time because they just don't know what might happen tomorrow. One serious earthquake and they're all gone.
- You start talking like they. But it's not true. - Mark disagreed – They live one day at the time because they don't have another choice. You see, they dream that one day a career will open for them and they'll be the movie stars and celebrities. Meanwhile though, they do nothing to empower themselves and increase their chances for that to happen. Drugs and alcohol only keep them away from achieving anything. This isn't life. It's a waiting room.
- Say what you want, but Sunset Boulevard is full of life. – Andrzej said.
- You call it a life? Love for money, friends for money, conversations about money. Does this sound like life to you?

They left their car and walked inside the place. In spite of the cigarette smoke and the smell of beer, the place seemed pleasantly inviting. They sat at the bar and ordered a beer.

- Look – Andrzej said – there's a pool table. Want to shoot a game?
- Wait a minute, we just sat down and you already get hyper.
- I sure do. It's been so long since I've played. I want to know if I lost my grip yet.

As they played, a tall guy in his thirties came up to them; long hair, leather jacket, dark sunglasses – a typical bar personality. He asked Andrzej:

- Do you want to shoot?
- Why not? – Andrzej answered with a smile.
- Twenty bucks for a win.

Andrzej looked at Mark, who gestured "NO" with his head.

- OK, deal – Andrzej sad – But only two games.

The stranger nodded and the two came up to the pool table and started to play. Mark sat at the bar table and watched them. At some point he heard a voice behind his back:

- Excuse me; can I sit down here?

He looked behind and saw a girl; tall, beautiful long, curly hair. Her gentle tan and toned down make up made huge impression on Mark.

- Sure, sit down.
- You have such nice accent; where are you from?
- From Poland.

- Oh, Poland. That's somewhere in Europe, isn't it?
- Yes – Mark answered thinking, "Yes, you dumb princess". He started telling her his immigrant experience. Meanwhile the situation at the pool table became tense.
- I don't know what's wrong with me today. I can't make a simple shot. – the stranger was getting mad.
- Don't trip, it'll get better. – Andrzej tried to cheer his pool buddy.
- Maybe it will, but not today. I'm done. – He dropped his stick and came up to Andrzej.
- It looks like you've won.
- I was just lucky. – Andrzej answered with humbleness.
- No, you play well and deserve your reward. – He pulled out a twenty dollars bill and handed it to Andrzej.
- Come on, let me buy you a beer – Andrzej said.
- No, thanks. I don't drink. – The strangers waved his hand in a good-bye gesture and left. Andrzej stood there surprised; the guy looked like a tough guy who had been around quite a bit yet his manners said that he was intelligent and honest.
- Who was this guy? – he asked the bartender.
- I don't know his name but he comes in here often. Some say that he writes music for the movies.

- Andrzej – Mark yelled – Come over
  here and meet the angel.

Andrzej came to the table and greeted the
girl, whose name turned out to be "Angel".

- This name fits you so well – Andrzej
  said – I wonder if you are a part of the
  City of Angels or if the city was built
  for you and for you only. How much
  time did God need to create such
  beauty? Perhaps you're not God's
  creature but were made by
  imagination of poets and painters?
  My name is Andrzej – he finally
  introduced himself. – I'm from
  Poland, land where neighbor respects
  his neighbor. In Poland bread is holy
  and work gets utmost respect, ladies
  get a kiss on their hand and children
  do not raise their voice when talking
  to parents. You are worthy of the
  greatest respect and love, and I'd be
  the happiest guy if I could be kissing
  your hands.

The girls listened to is as Mark was sitting
stunned – it was the first time in his life he
heard his brother pay complements to a
woman in such romantic spur of passion.
What's more – he wasn't lying and it
showed.

- I do admit that I don't know anything
  about Poland but as I listen to you I
  promise that soon I'll learn about
  your country as much as you know
  already.

196

Mark thought, "She's not as dumb as I thought". Andrzej grabbed her hand and said:

- That's so nice of you to want to learn about my country. I'll be happy to help.
- With a guy like you I can study for the rest of my life.

Andrzej embraced her without saying a word and she rest her head on his shoulder.

- Ok, kids – Andrzej interrupted – take me home and then you can do whatever you want.

Just like a wave of the sea reaches the shore and comes back
So has my love reached me but confined like lava.
Here, in this land of millions dancing to music and rhythms, which are like bridges
I met her – more dear than the dream, I met the girl among the sweet oranges.
She fills my nights with love,
Brightens my life's each day
Wouldn't you like to know her name?
Well, let me tell you: it's Angel.

Andrzej put away his guitar and kissed Angela.

- I put it together for you – he said.
- I thank you. I liked it very much. You know, my dad likes you very much too.
- I think I can consider this great news – he said and rejoiced.

- Definitely, usually he doesn't like me to go out with anybody. Plus he got you a job.
- What job? –Andrzej asked very surprised.
- You'll be delivering luggage to the airport. It pays 8.5 per hour plus you'll get health insurance and benefits.

Andrzej almost jumped, he was so happy.
- No more welding! – he screamed – Come on, let's celebrate by the ocean.

They sat in Angela's small convertible VW and drove away towards Santa Monica. The sunset was absolutely gorgeous. People walked along the beach while small clusters of friends looked up and admired the beautiful horizon. Andrzej and Angela kissed passionately on the sand. Gentle sound of ocean water resounded like the chorus of a love song.
- You know what? – Angela whispered – I want to be with you always.

Andrzej listened to her words but they weren't getting there, his mind was in Poland, by the Baltic. The sunset reminded him of his school years, the friends he had made and girls he had hugged. He wasn't sure if it was missing or just a picture cut out from his memory. Thoughts: "Angela – she is an American. She'll never understand what it is that I'm feeling. Yet… it feels so good to be with her. I see, she wants to understand me.
I have to help her…"
After a moment he "woke up".

- I'm sorry, I didn't hear what you said.
- I said "I love you". You know, I understand that is must not be easy for you to just forget your friends, perhaps there is even a girl you liked left there. I don't want you to forfeit this, those memories. I just want you to know that I do love you. O, I don't want you to say the same. I know that if that's the case, you'll tell me...

Andrzej was looking in her eyes hoping to see something that would take him away from the magical feeling. Nothing... "I love you, but I won't tell you this" – he thought.

A beautiful, sunny day and the music on the radio put Mark in a great mood on the way from work. "Angela truly is great – he thought – it's been four months and I've never seen her unhappy yet. Always full of energy, smile. It would be so good if Andrzej treated her seriously. A wedding would be so good, once Angela comes with the children".

He exited the freeway and took Van Nuys street. He pulled by a gas station and while pumping the gas he heard a woman speaking Russia. He looked around and saw her – maybe in her forties, dressed casually but carefully, which gave her a look of a business owner.

- How do you do? – Mark asked in Russian.
- Good, how'bout you? - She answered looking at him ith interest and added:
- Where are you from?

- Detroit.
- Oh, my God! It's full of Blacks down tere. Lucky you're alive.
- It's not that bad – he said.
- Where were you born?
- Poland.
- Poland! Do you want to work for me?
- What would I do and for how much?
- Pump gas in cars, wash windshields, check oil. Five bucks per hour plus you get to keep whatever the tips.

Mark was thinking about he offer. He's had it enough on construction. Her offer wasn't too hot either but it didn't require hard physical labor. He agreed under condition that he gets to keep is Sundays off.

As they were talking his attention focused on a gorgeous dog of the owner – the Siberian shepherd. Its red fur had a particular shine in the Sun. Its eyes had a solid black color. Pinto was the dog's name and it like Mark from the very beginning. He could pet Pinto and wiggled the tail constantly.

- Pinto, are we friends, or what? - Mark said while getting into his car and took off in the best mood ever.

Warm California days go by fast. Both f the brothers were very happy with the jobs they had and with their "mom", who cared for them both dearly. "Mom was Angela, of course". She visited Andrzej and Mark at work and usually brought some goodies to eat. Saturday and Sunday she took them for getaways to various places. Even her dad would occasionally meet them for beer and spend time. Angela's mother passed away of cancer a few years after she had had Angela. Ever since Angela was the lady of the house. Mark got a letter from his wife that things related to her coming to America were approaching the final stage. Soon they'll all be together. Andrzej started going to a Polish church for mass from time to time, which made Mark feel very happy. As it turned out, however, it wasn't just the religious needs but also the charm of Sister Elizabeth, which were to blame for Andrzej's Christian awakening. Mark meanwhile, was pleased with the results of training that Pinto was getting. He could talk for hours how he tought the dog to give a paw, lay down, etc. Angela ave the brothers a gift: t-shiorts saying "AMAF" – Angela, Andrzej, Mark, Forever.

Mark was sitting in a recliner in front opf the entranmce to the gas station. Inside the owner was counting money. The day was as usual – sunny and nice. Traffic at the station was close to none. N the opposite side of the street a Black man was riding is bike. He crossed the stop sign and stopped at the station's parking lot. All of the sudden Pinto took off barking towards the guy. Mark got up off his chair ad came up to the owner saying:
-    I asked you not to teach your dog to attack the Black people.

- It's not your dog and none of your business. If someone were to rub us then you'd say "thank you".
- It well may be, but that Black guy was just passing by and there is Pinto right next to him in a matter of seconds showing the teeth.
- Leave me alone. I am really busy.

The man meanwhile jumped off of his bike and grabbed a metal broom sitting next to the gas pump. He aimed at the dog and Pinto scared backed off but only to rush back against the guy in a second. The guy hit: once, twice. Pinto squealed, turned around and rushed towards the office. The man did not give up just yet and followed the dog. Seeing what was going on, the owner hid the money and left outside. The man ran up to her and yelled:

- Is this your dog?
- No. I have no idea where it came from.
- I'll kill the beast. – the man yelled and headed for the office where Pinto was laying down.
- Don't touch it! It's my dog! – Mark shouted.

But the man wasn't listening and stormed into the office and with a broom started to torture the animal.

Pinto squealed as if asking for help. Mark wanted to get in there to stop the guy but the owner stopped him instead.

- Don't go in there. The cops will come and we'll be in a lot of trouble.

202

This dude can sue us and we ca lose a
fortune.
-    Well, what about Pinto?
The owner didn't answer. Pinto was fighting
for his life and managed to make it in
between legs of the attacker. He rushed out
on the street and stumbling ran to the park.
The guy, all sweaty, dropped the broom, got
on his bike and left. The owner followed him
with her eyes and once he was out of sight
she said:t
-    It's a good thing I ended that way.
Mark could not believe the whole thing.
-    What did you say? "It's a good thing
     it ended that way? This dog now has
     broken legs. If you gave the black a
     hundred bucks this all wouldn't have
     happened.
-    You don't know America yet.
     Besides, Pinto will come back.
Mark looked in her eyes and asked:
-    Would you come back?
The owner didn't feel like discussing it any
further. She sat in her Mercedes and took
off. Mark, meanwhile, stayed on the parking
lot and with tears in his eyes stared in
direction of the park. "Pinto, come back. I'll
take you far away from here' – he thought.
The thoughts were traveling through
corridors of his mind; "What a racist bitch.
You raise your dog just to betray him at the
end, just to shit on friendship and love. For
what, for pennies?" and out loud he said:
"Judas, not a woman".
He went to the office, turned off the
electricity and closed up the pomps. On the

paking lot he put the sign: "Station closed".
He locked the door and threw the key to the
sewer. On the door he posted a sign: "I left,
but you know well that I'll be back – just like
Pinto".
Mark never came back to work at the gas
station. Adrzej, on the other hand, quite
moved by the whole occurrence often
ooffered: "Let's go there. I'll beat the shit
out of her". With time however, he came to
the conslusion that the owner wasn't worthy
their attention any more. She was wealthy
but she didn't own any money – it owned
her.

This morning the brothers were sitting
accompanied by Jola and Angela. They were
trying to teach Angela some Polish. Andrzej
tried a difficult task – he wanted to explain
the difference between Polish words, which
sound just very close and mean: "we wash",
"you eat", "and you squeal". There was so
much laughter going on with it. It was
around midnight, when they finished their
language discussions and sat on the bench
filling up the glasses with wine. They were
making plans for the future. Angela took a
piece of paper out of her purse and asked
everyone to be quiet. She started to read:

Sitting on the beach my eyes were glued to
the view of the sea
Nothing, however, nothing but the boy from
Poland – that's all I can see
Like foaming waves my minds drifted
through Hollywood

Through L.A., through Santa Monica, but
they'd always come back.
I asked the magician – who is that man?
That man, who cuts my heart in pieces, who
is like an eternal wound
I'll tell you my dear, his first name is
Andrzej, the surname – Polskowicz.

She ended, got up and bowed. Both brothers
and Jola as well started to applaud.
-      You see, I can try poetry myself.
-      Can tell. I'm very proud of you.
Mark wanted to say something but at the
same moment he felt the floor shake very
strong. The glassware fell on the ground and
the chandelier started to swing. Andrzej
screamed:
-      What is it, for heaven's sake?
-      It's an earthquake – Angela answered
       – Quickly, have to stand by the
       doorframes.
Andrzej and Jola quickly jumped towards the
door but Mark chose to stand by the window.
-      What are you doing? – Andrzej yelled
       at him – Come here quickly.
But he wasn't listening. Looking through the
window he saw the street rock, cars jumping
swinging to the left and right like plants
moved by the wind. "Unbelievable" – he
thought.
The earthquake stopped and they started to
pick up the pieces of the broken glass. Jola
was wiping the wine of the floor and Angela
said with a smile:
-      You have just gone through your
       California baptismal. Now you can

officially say that you know life in this state.
- Nice baptismal – Andrzej responded - There is no point in running away since there really isn't many places to run for.
- This wasn't too much of an earthquake – Angela continued – It will happen again in a few minutes but will be much weaker. Clean up her and I'll go and see if everything is all right at home and with my dad. I'll see you tomorrow.

Angela was right – the shaking reoccurred but not with so much strength anymore. The brothers were watching news on TV and to their surprise there was just brief information that nothing serious besides some freeway damage happened. Mark said:
- Now I understand why do they live one day at the time
- You're exaggerating. Have some wine and think what will we do tomorrow.

Andrzej came home straight from work. Jola was fixing something to eat and Mark watched the people pass by on the street.
- Nobody even mentioned anything about the earthquake at work – Andrzej said- I guess they think of it as of a minor shower or something.
- Nothing really collapsed so why the fuzz? - Jola said.
- Was Angela at work? – Mark asked.
- Good thing you mention. I was just about to call her and see what

happened – she always comes to see me during the lunch break.

- Maybe something came up – Jola said.
- So what are we doing with the whole L.A. situation? I mean, wecan't just keep on living at Jola's. Aneta is going to come soon with the kids. I have to make sure they have everything they need. – Mark asked.
- You're right. On one hnd life here truly is great; gateways to the beach, the mountains, great weather almost all the time. But I've been checking out the prices of homes and honestly Detroit is like half cheaper. Taxes in L.A. are also much higher and in general I think you should come back to Detroit – Andrzej responded.
- What about you? – Mark asked his brother.
- I'll wait a while yet because I have to take care of some things with mee and Angela.
- "Take care of some things?" – Mark got nosy.
- All right, I'll tell you. I didn't know how for a long time but I guess I'll just say that her and I have planned to start to live together. She was supposed to talk to her father today.
- That's great! – Mark said excited – Don't worry about me – even if I am to go back to Detroit, we'll still be visiting each other. Mom will also be

happy to know that you finally decided to stick with one girlfriend.

- So, you wouldn't be mad at me?
- Why would I?
- I feel so much better. I'm going to call Angela to let her know that everything is all right.

Andrzej picked up the phone and dialed the number. Once he got connected he moved to another room.

Soon this crazy life of yours will be over – Jola said to Mark – But it's a good thing. Finally you'll have some stability in life; family, kids – it will straighten Andrzej big time.

Mark yelled to Andrzej;

- What's taking you so long?
- Leave him alone – Jola intervened – Let them plan everything; where to live, etc.

After a few minutes Andrzej left the room. He was totally pale; just stood in the middle of the room not saying anything.

- What's this about? Did Angela ask you to marry her, or what? – Mark asked jokingly.
- Last night – Andrzej started – when she left our place she got on the freeway. She wasn't speeding or anything. She was on the right lane when she ran into one of the wholes left after the earthquake. She lost control and hit the left median wall. The two cars that were on the opposite side of traffic didn't make it to stop. They hit her tiny VW. The

ambulance came and took her to the
hospital.
- Oh God, how is she doing? Is she
  going to be ok? – Jola screamed.
- She died this morning – Andrzej said
  quietly.

L.A, as usually, was full of life; millions of
people running here and there, the ocean's
waves hitting the shore in never changing
rhythm, clusters of children building their
sand construction projects, just an ordinary
California day. Nobody seemed to even
notice that a girl from the "land of oranges"
was missing.
It was a long goodbye between Jola and the
two brothers. All in all they spent together
nine months. After Angela's funeral the boys
decided to go back to Detroit. The beautiful
weather, the ocean and gardens always
staying green, the story of Angela, Pinto and
such made California just not so happy
anymore. Andrzej changed the tires, the
same ones that he got in Denver, Mark did all
the necessary shopping and they took off;
towards San Francisco, then through Idaho
and Montana they reached South Dakota and
Wisconsin. They left Los Angeles early in
the morning. Mark was humming his
favorite song and Andrzej without a word
was staring ahead. San Francisco welcomed
them with beautiful Sun. They passed the
Golden Gate and watched the Alcatraz island
pass by. They watched the impressive
skyscrapers, which seemed to almost teas the
world and say: in spite of the tragic

209

earthquake in 1906, the city lives and blossoms. By the evening they left San Francisco only to face once again the deserts of Nevada.

They switched driving back and forth. This time, not knowing why, they really wanted to get to Detroit as quickly as possible. To their surprise the northeastern part of Nevada, called the "Jarbidge Wilderness" differed completely from the monotonous overall view of the state. Sixty-five thousands of acres of green meadows and were just filled with flowers. They even didn't have time to see the entire lively flower scene as suddenly they already were in Idaho. "Grem State" as it is often referred to, means precious stones state. Some seventy different kinds of stones with 10 and a half carat diamond were found there. The brothers traveled through the mountains and through the prairies looking at muddy areas and crop fields, and the breathtaking waterfalls called the "twins" spread at the foot of the Snake River. Water falling from seventy meters height spanned. Everything seemed to be telling the history of his wild place. Wyoming, on the other hand, welcomed them with steam and the geysers bursting out. They drove fast but tried hard to get to see at least some signs of human existence here; unsuccessfully. The farms were separated from each other with the belt of lakes, mountains and prairies. Right before the Montana border they had to stop. Huge clouds brought down the pouring rain to the area they were driving through. Hail of the size of a tennis ball bombarded the car.

Wind speeding 120 kilometers per hour was ripping out smaller size trees throwing them around. The brothers tried to protect the glass windshields but not all of them survived the angry storm. Once the hail stopped they took off almost panicking. They wanted to get out of this wild and forgotten place.
They entered South Dakota and in spite of the beautiful weather there was something in the air tat bothered them.

- It is much better here than in Montana – Mark said.
- Yeah, that hail could have killed us. But I still feel strange.
- You know, me too, but maybe it's just us being oversensitive after all the storms and winds.
- I don't think so. Look at the sky. It's clear blue but if you look closely at the mountain peaks you see something like shadows going by. Where are the shadows coming from if there are no clouds?

They kept on driving in silence; passed the beautiful tract from which to admire the faces of the Presidents, carved in stonewall. They were driving east and soon they noticed the different kinds of stones. The most interesting thing though, was that the stones formations themselves had different colors. Some of them started off with dark blue stripes, then picked up some white-green and red to orange, and finished with green and yellow ones. Mark called those hills "the rainbow mountain", which perfectly gave away the character of the scenario.

211

- Good thing the front windshield is intact – Mark said.
- We'd have been screwed. It would feel like riding a motorbike or something. You know, overall we were lucky. I was sure the hail would just crush everything.
- Andrzej look, the motor temp is rising.

Andrzej looked at the dashboard.

- It's not so bad. Maybe there's some water missing in the radiator but we'll make it to the next town.
- I just don't want any surprises.
- Don't worry. They checked the engine in L.A. and everything was good.

They kept on driving while listening to the music. They wanted to reach Minnesota that same day. Suddenly the car severely slowed down. From underneath the hood unidentifiable noise started to grumble as if instead of pistons somebody was simply banging with a hammer. Inside the car they could smell the burning oil. They drove to the shoulder.

- Well, that would be it – Mark summed it up.
- Stop whining – Andrzej was checking the oil level - Look; particles of metal on oil. Looks like we killed the motor.
- What do you mean, "killed the motor" – Mark asked.
- What I mean is we can't drive anymore – Andrzej was getting mad.

212

- How did it happen?
- I don't know but apparently the indicators were faulty. They kept showing the right temp and the right oil level.
- Do you remember how long it took in Colorado for somebody to finally stop and give us a ride?
- I do, but there's nothing we can do and we have to get to the nearest town.

Traffic on the freeway was slow. One could even say that there was no traffic. They waited patiently as they had no other choice. There was some thirty miles to the nearest town. In spite of very strong Sun the temperatures started to drop and the dry, frosty wind started to beam against their faces. They had to put their winter jackets on. After four hours a car appeared on the horizon. It got closer and slowed down but they didn't even try to stop it since all of their previous attempts ended up with nothing. But the car surprisingly stopped. It was an old, beat up van, so covered with mud it was hard to see what color was it. A person came out from behind the wheel; it was a short, well bilt man with long, black hair to his shoulders. He stopped on the sholder and with a strange accent asked:

- Where do you guys need to get to?

Two brothers looked at each other with a smile and Mark answered:

- To the nearest town.

They guy came back to his car looking for something and after a moment threw a rope to Andrzej.

- Hook it up.

Andrzej did exactly what he was told and they got in their car. After a moment they felt a gentle pull and they knew they were being towed.

- Did you take a look at that guy? – Mark asked.
- Yeah, he looks like an Indian.
- I wonder what's he doing here.
- What you mean? He probably lives somewhere here.
- On this desert?
- And what did you think, that all Indians live in L.A.? – Andrzej laughed – these are their original territories. They're at home and we're the invaders.

After a while the brothers started to notice shadows of some buildings. As they got closer they realized that the place they had arrived to could hardly be called a village; four, maybe five houses one almost next to the other, no asphalt or sidewalks resembled more of a camp. Right by the road there was a small, one story house surrounded by trashcans. It turned out to be a local store where one could buy everything. They stopped the car on sandy parking spot near the store and Mark tried to pay the Indian for favor. He, however, definitely refused.

- You always have to help the one in need – he said and disappeared behind the buildings.

214

- Come on; let's check the store out and ask if there is some service station nearby - Andrzej said. They walked in and the nice interior was rich in variety of products. From basic groceries one could also purchase circles and saws. Shotguns and ammunition was laid out right by the entrance.
- Look at all this – Mark shouted to Andrzej.
- All that's missing is arrows and spears – Andrzej said with a smile. At the same time a guy from behind the counter said:\
- Here we don't talk jokingly about guns.

There would be nothing strange about it if it weren't for the fact that the voice said it in Polish. The two brothers looked at each other with disbelief. Andrzej yelled:
- Hallo, Sir; do you speak Polish?
- Of course I do – the man replied and walked out from behind the counter – I came to this area right after the war. It was hard at the beginning but with time I fell in love with it and so I've stayed here till today. The Indians like me too, and I even had an Indian wife. She died six years ago. My children didn't want to stay here. They got the taste of the city and moved. My son lives in Chicago and my daughter in New York. I do have to say though, that you surprised me big time; I have not heard the Polish

language in years. The Indians are good people but you have to be careful what you say. Don't ever laugh at their customs make comments about them and their behavior. The second thing is: stay away from their girls. If men let you speak to women then fine, otherwise keep quiet.

The man placed a finger on his lips as he said that. Andrzej asked:

- What about our car? Is there some place where we could fix it here?
- I'm sorry, really, but the closest city is Sioux City. Now they out there don't want to send their mechanics over here. I don't even think they would send a tow truck.
- So what we're gonna do?
- I have a phone in the back. Come with me and we'll give it a shot with few places.
- What is your name? – Andrzej kept asking.
- My name is Zygmunt Konieczny. Where in Poland are you from, boys?
- Bydgoszcz.
- Wow! I was born in Chojnice.
- Mark, you go and make the calls and I will get something to celebrate this amazing meeting with Mr. Zygmunt.

Mark was calling the Sioux City while Andrzej and Zygmunt sat on the bench and drank beer. Andrzej was talking about life in Poland. Zygmunt was introducing him to the mysterious and amazing tales of life of the Sioux in Dakota.

After some time Andrzej noticed that more and more Indians were coming out of their places. They were walking up to the store ad sitting next to him without even asking for permission. They were reaching to his bag and getting the beer out of it and drank, listening to conversations about Poland. At some point Zygmunt stopped speaking Polish giving Andrzej the idea that they had guests. Andrzej understood and himself started to speak English. The Indians on the other hand realized that the Poles accepted their company. They felt more comfortable and asked Andrzej about Poland and about life in L.A. It made him feel good; for the first time in a long time someone was actually listening to what he had to say. Not only that; his life story was listened to with a great deal of attention. The Indians paid attention to the smallest detail and it was easy to see that they lived through his ups and downs. His life started to have a meaning as opposed to Los Angeles, where he was just a particle of huge agglomeration, unknown to anybody just a money maker. In this wild land he was somebody he always wanted to be – a human being, someone with the heart and feelings, a person with a dream, with disappointments. Once he finished his story the Indians commented on it with understanding. The nice atmosphere was interrupted by Mark's arrival:

- Nothing, not even will move a finger to fix my car. Is everybody a millionaire by now? I mean I don't want anything for free.

- Sit down here, bro and have abeer with us. Relax and we'll figure something out tomorrow.
- I'm afraid we won't come up with anything tomorrow. Even if someone took our car, it would take like two weeks to get the engine fixed. How do you imagine it here, in the middle of the prairie, among the Indians, with no hotel or a restaurant?
- You can stay at my place – Zygmunt said.
- No way – Mark protested – I've made the decision already. We'll take a bus and to hell with this car. I'll get another one.

He reached for the beer, opened it and drank quickly. An older Indian man said to him:

- Don't get mad.

Mark stopped drinking and looked at the group of Indians sitting across from him. All of them with long, black hair, dark complexion – they all looked very much alike. Mark asked:

- How can I not get angry? Do you have a solution?
- No, I don't. But it seems to me that you don't really need a solution.
- What is that supposed to mean?
- Just a moment ago you said you had already made your mind. So if you've made a decision already there's no more problem. I don't see

why getting upset over something that no longer is.

Mark looked at him surprised and thought: "Honestly, he's got a point. I should start learning how to treat problems this way. The Indian guy asked him:

- How much did you spend for the tires?
- 250 dollars.

The Native American came up to him and handed him 250 dollars.

- What is that for? – Mark asked.
- For your tires. If you plan to leave this car here tomorrow, I want the right to your tires.

Mark didn't think much.

- The tires are yours.
- Thank you. Now not only you don't have a problem anymore but also you've made 250 bucks. Good day overall.

Mark wanted to say something, as he liked very much the guy's approach. He sat there quietly and kept telling himself what a successful day it was. After a while he walked up to the Indian and said:

- Thanks for what you did for me today.

All other Indians looked at Mark and the silence surrounded them all. The guy stopped it y saying:

- Now you talk like one of us.

The rest started to clap, whistle and scream in excitement. Andrzej and Mark started to do the same thing and the party began. As time went y the Indians allowed Mark and Andrzej to talk to women as well. It was an amazing thing for the brothers. As they talked to the girls they noticed how different their life viewpoints were. Indian women didn't talk at all about the house, cars, furniture or clothes. Instead they stressed how important it was for them how the men will treat them and how they will treat the men. Andrzej concluded:

Well, maybe one day I will go back to Dakota to find a wife.

Mark was sitting with the elder Indian guy and asked him a lot of questions regarding nature.

- How is it possible that the sky is clear blue and yet there are like shadows traveling through stonewalls?
- You have to learn the taste of the distance, the smell of silence, which can only be stopped by the wind. Then in the worshipped mountains you will see the Great Spirit of the Sioux, the last two hundred of whom died in 1890, after fifteen years of war with the white men. It is him, who travels through the land of Dakota praising the names of the fallen heroes.

Mark listened to this story with disbelief. He only saw such things in movies, but never though this could actually happen in reality. The next day they boarded the bus. The Indians and Zygmunt waived their long goodbye. And so, the next page in the book of history of their trip turned over. They were on their way to Sioux City. The bus was full; women with children and lots of packages were talking loudly, smoking cigarettes. At the back of the bus two Indian guys were drinking whiskey and from time to time making sure that their "luggage" – that being small crates containing live chickens and rabbits – was ok. Andrzej laughed hysterically.

-    What a circus! – he kept repeating.
In Sioux City they transferred to a modern bus where passengers were totally different too. The Indian women and drunken men were no longer. The colorful costumes were replaced with blue jeans and T-shirts advertising popular brands. There was no smoking and children sat quietly preoccupied with electronic games.

They passed by cold Minnesota and arrived to Wisconsin. The state of pouring milk and honey didn't impress the two boys, however. Mark compared it to the familiar parts of Poland; planes with farms, occasionally interrupted by forests and lakes. Time was passing by very slowly on the bus and in spite of their many unfortunate adventures they talked about them with true joy.

They've been to seventeen states; each one had its own, original charm. Once they got back to Chicago they felt like they were coming home, which they still didn't have but they felt they were a part of mid-west America. No palm trees, or ocean waves stayed in their minds but pine trees and willows, and oaks as if overlooking the Vistula River. That's why Michigan just felt so much more like home to them. Entering

221

Detroit they looked with pleasure at dirty streets and old uncared for houses. The Polish Hamtramck had unexpectedly a positive impact on both of them.

They looked differently at stores that had Polish signs and the club in the east part of town looked different too. Mark asked his brother:

- Is it just me or things simply got prettier here?
- I don't think they did. I think it's us who now has a different perspective on things.

For how long can one live waiting for something? The lonely nights, mornings with no voices of children playing… Hours spent at work run day by day faster and faster. A lonely man is never in a hurry, just sometimes asks God to prolong some of the minutes. Why hurry when no one is waiting? Why effort, when there's no one trying to profit from it? Where is the borderline of waiting, behind, which memories fade away? Places and persons with whom we felt such bond once, now make up a shapeless figure, pushed on by the arms of a clock. We forget the past not because we want to disattach ourselves from it. It is the tiredness caused by memories that makes us disattach ourselves from it.

After two years of separation Mark finally got to witness his family's arrival. The welcome at the airport only at first glance seemed stereotypical. Aneta held Mark's handand the kids were telling him stories from Poland. Andrzej took care of the luggage and after a short while everybody was home. Mark and Andrzej no longer lived together and Andrzej let Mark rent half of the house to Aneta and the children. He himself lived with his bar buddy, Henio. Mark talked with Aneta for a long time; about the parents and the situation in the country. Mark loved spending his time with the children who grew up significantly. After a short time everyone started to act like in the old days and it was hard to guess that they had not seen each other for two years. Aneta unpacked the luggage and children with great interest watched the American cartoons. Mark and Andrzej like back in the days had their beers and talked about work a lot. Children playing, Aneta in the kitchen and scents of food brought back the familiar atmosphere. Aneta's remarks on the layout of the flat and lack of closet space always caused two brothers to laugh. Two years ago they too, in almost an identical manner criticized the same things in pani Jadzia's house. They still could not afford new furniture or nice home decorations. Small TV, used futon and an armchair was all they really had. But the most important was that they were together and building the future was now up to them. Neither Aneta nor the kids had any idea about the metro Detroit structure. She didn't know about the large palaces with marble floors and crystal chandeliers, and golden doorknobs just a few miles north west of where they lived.

Garages of those rich areas where larger than their house and the cars shined with freshness and luxury. Mark knew it well by now and from time to time it bothered him that he couldn't give his family the "real America".

Mark's new job was very different to the one he had before. He now worked in a warehouse, from which WIERTLA were sent out all over the world. At the beginning he loved it. He was taking orders from Sweden, Germany, France, Taiwan and Hong Kong. With time, however, monotony came in to daily activities. Sometimes he watched the other two Poles who worked in the same factory. They were TOKARZE from Poland, working in production. He'd spend time with them during breaks talking about the situation in the company and gossiping about other employees and owners.

- What do you do for the weekend? – Stasio, one of them, asked.
- I don't really have any plans – Mark answered.
- Why don't you come to my place? Bring your wife and the kids.
- That sounds good. Where do you live?
- In Sterling Heights, some 15 miles north from where you're at.
- How long have you lived there?
- Six years. At first I lived in Hamtramck, like you. With time things were getting better and finally we could afford a new house.
- How long have you worked here?

- It's going to be 17 years.
- Wow! Seventeen years in the same place? Why didn't you try something else? Maybe you'd be doing even better.
- You know how it is. I have three kids. My wife couldn't really work because she had to take care of them. Working here, by the machine, I didn't really have to know English. Years went by and my English stayed where it always has been. Now the kids are about to finish high school. I have to help them once they start college.
- Where do you go for vacation?
- Oh, vacation is always a great time. My wife and me either go to Poland or to Florida.
- Do you go often?
- What do you mean by "often"?
- I mean like how many times a year do you go?
- Are you crazy? We only can go maybe once a year, and no more than two or three weeks.

The break was over and Stasio and Mark had to return to work. Mark thought: "Seventeen years y the machine and he gets to see the world once a year for two or three weeks". On Saturday the Polskowicz family paid Stasio a visit. His house was quite spacey; three medium size bedrooms upstairs, dinning room and living room downstairs. A well taken care of garden in the back yard added to the charm. With American custom,

225

Stasio started the grill and put some pork chops on. The wives talked about the children and Mark told the kids how to tell the difference between birds in the garden. It was atypical Saturday afternoon. Stasio's wife asked Aneta:

- So how do you like it here, in America?
- I still don't know if I like it or not. But I know I miss Poland. Life here is different, definitely. Everyone just takes care of themselves. Mark has changed a bit himself too.
- It's normal. My husband loved going fishing or picking mushrooms. Once we bought this house all he does is work, work, work. And when he has an afternoon of he just fixes things around the house. We used to go to the movies sometimes. Now there's just no time for anything.
- I wouldn't mind having a nice house. But I would not want to bee its slave.
- Girls! – Stasio yelled – Get the table ready. The food is almost done.

Andrzej was sitting in the Polish bar with a friend whom he had met short time before. Konrad – that was his name – worked for a company that fixed telephones and radio TV equipment. They got to talk about it because it was Andrzej's field. He was out of his country for three years yet never got to working in his field of electronics. Konrad, on the other and, needed just someone like him. He had a plan. Besides the professional

226

interests they also had many other subjects in common; music, jokes, polish memories also from the school years. But the most important common ground was for both of them "making money". They talked for hours about possibilities of opening their own business but usually words was everything that came out of those conversations. This time, however, Konrad was serious. He knew that his plan could work. So they walked away from the bar and sat at the table. Konrad started:

- The GTE company used to make telephones. But as time went by they become more and more popular and so they, instead of selling them, started to rent them to the customers. After a year or two, people would return them. Times changed again and technology moved forward; nobody wanted to rent phones with a cable anymore because the cordless ones started to enter the market. GTE therefore stopped producing their phones. One problem remained, however – what to do with those phones that people were still returning to the company? And here is where we enter the stage – we contact the GTE and buy off their used phones.
- Why would you want some used telephones? – Andrzej didn't understand.
- Everybody thinks just the way you do. Yet nobody knows that these

phones are still working or they just
need to change a small part or two.
- OK, then what?
- Then we clean them really good, paint
them and in a new box sell it at a
lower price.
- All right, to whom and for how
much?
- We'll make an offer to GTE; two
bucks per phone. We'll lose – say –
two bucks to fix one but once the
product is ready we'll sell it for ten.
What do you think?
- It sounds good, but my English still
isn't at the point where I can negotiate
with GTE.
- That's why there will be the two of
uus; you will take care of the "fixing"
issue and the whole production and I
will take care of GTE and potential
buyers. Deal?
- Deal – Andrzej said without thinking
much. They shok their hands and
clinked the beer mugs.
- How are we going to name our
company?
Andrzej sat quiet for a while, then whispered
something to himself, as if pronouncing some
magical words. Finally he said:
- We're both from Europe and the
nature of the business will be
electronics, so how do you like the
name "Eurotonics"?
- Fantastic! Let it be "Eurotonics".

Ania and Janek sat on the grass in the garden. Mark was telling some made up stories about super skilled rabbits and very strong bears, the princesses and brave knights. Kids loved it when their dad was introducing them into this magical world of tales. Mark loved those moments as well. He saw interest on his children's faces; sometimes with laughter and sometimes with fear they would ask:
"Daddy, did it happen for real?"
Isn't it great when children listen to our stories? It is one of those times when we can say with full satisfaction and confidence that our words were not spoken in veins. This sweet relation between the listener and the talker – wouldn't we wish for it to just stay forever?
As the time flies the magical tales lose its charm. Nobody asks anymore whether what we said was true.

- I decided to change jobs – Mark announced.
- Why? – Aneta asked.
- Because what I'm doing now has to be thee most boring job there is.
- What do you plant to do?
- I'll start cleaning homes and offices. With time I'll hire some girls and if things go well I'll get some offices in town. It should work out.
- It may, but how are we going to live? You're not going to make money from day one.
- You always see some problems and the thing is to find the right solution

229

instead of looking constantly for additional obstacles.

- Well, so what is your solution?
- See, there you go again. By asking me what solution I have, you keep asking the same question – how will we survive without money? It sounds different but has the same meaning.
- What if I go to work, just for the time you establish that business of yours.
- Now you're talking. But I already have an idea. I'll by a beat up or crashed car at the auction, fix it and sell it. It should be enough to start.
- So why the whole fuss about "finding solution" - Aneta got impatient.
- Because I want you to be a part of success, not just a viewer.
- What if things don't work out?
- See, again! You just came back to the first question.

Andrzej and Konrad left McDonald's where they got a burger and milk shake. They got in their car and took off.

- You did great with GTE – Mark said with excitement.
- Maybe it was just luck.
- Don't be so shy. They were really glad to get rid off those phones.
- Maybe you're right, they seemed to be pleased. One thing is sure – we can start.
- You've cleaned the car nicely.

- It took me like an hour. It was saw dirty you could barely see the windshield
- Now on the other hand it looks like it doesn't have the windshields.
- By the way, since you've mentioned the car.
- What about it?
- Don't you think you always bring me bad luck whenever you ride with me. Two days ago the radiator broke. That same evening we lost the whole wheel for no apparent reason. A week ago the front hood opened up right in the middle of the freeway...

Andrzej couldn't hold it anymore and busted out laughing.
- It's not bad luck. It's a sign for you that the time came to change the vehicle.
- Say whatever you want but I like this car a lot.
- Well, then keep on driving it but don't blame it on me that I "bring you bad luck".
- All right, all right. Maybe you're right, it's just coincidences. – Konrad changed the subject – I don't like this milk, as if it were spoiled.
- Dump it then.

Konrad threw the cup forcefully and the white stream spilled out. At some point, however, it suddenly changed the very direction and "came back" covering both Andrzej and Konrad's clothes.

231

- You idiot, look what you did! - Andrzej screaned – Look at us now!
- I have no idea how it happened.
- I do – Andrzej said laughing – First you should open up the window and then throw it.
- Damn it, II though it was open. Shit, I cleaned it so nicely I couldn't tell whether it was shut or not.
- Now we look like we got jobs in milk factory. Pull over at this parking lot and let's clea up a bit.

Konrad made a turn towards the parking lot. Then: "thump" – the car made a noise.
- What the hell was that? – Andrzej asked.
- I don't know and I don't want to know.

"Thump" – the same noise.
- You better stop. We have to check what's going on.

They stopped , got out of the car and checked the underneath. After a moment Konrad yelled:
- Nice, that's the last thing I expected. The suspension is cracking!

Andrzej couldn't hold it and started to laugh hysterically. Tears started to pour out of his eyes he was laughing so hard. He asked Konrad:
- You still like this car?
- I piss on it. It won't even make sense to fix it. Let's just take the tags off and leave it here. Maybe somebody can use it.

Mark was following through with his plan vigorously. He bought a crashed car and sold it after he had fixed it making a decent profit. Then he drove for days with leaving fliers advertising his cleaning service. Soon first assignments started to come. His spare moments always were with the kids. He taught them roller blading and biking. They talked about school and new friends they've made. The demand for service from his company was growing and finally Mark hired some women. The company was doing great. With the increase of the number of clients so did increase the number of complaints. He liked and respected the women who worked for him. He knew he could count on them and was confident with their work. But when talking to clients he had to agree with them and it was hard to get used to saying words he didn't mean, "I apologize. Certainly, it was a misunderstanding. This won't happen again." etc. Soon thee words started to replace the other ones from his vocabulary. He realized that not everybody is fit t run a business like this. The initial successes and getting to know the market brought him a lot of satisfaction but as time went by the so-far interesting occupation became nothing but constant apologies to clients and reprimanding the employees. Reality differed from his dreams by far. He thought: "You can't please everyone. The funniest part is that people like it that way. Be it the client or the employee – each one will defend his point and no side is willing to compromise or loosen up. And all it takes is a little bit of good will". But the reality did not suggest that this would happen any time soon and some day he simply said to Aneta:

- I'll drop this business. To hell with it.
- But it took you so long to start it – Aneta answered somewhat shy.
- Too bad. I just can't keep listening to constant bitching. Sometimes I think that the girls feel like their working as punishment, while the clients that they do some huge favor to somebody. If that's the case then why either one side simply won't give up? And when they're done arguing between themselves they take their frustration on me.
- So what's going to happen next?
- What would you say we open a grocery store?
- And what would I be doing there?
- Helping.
- Oh no, I don't think this is a good idea.
- I know – Mark said finally – I expected it and so I'll do it alone.

Recession; as easy as it comes, so it goes away and people realize this. Nevertheless people don't ever seem to bee prepared for it. The years of prosperity weaken the self-preservation instinct. Time of confrontation comes; confrontation between the banks and those who owe them. Money borrowed easily is harder and harder to pay off and finally the moment comes when there's simply no way to pay them back. Rainy clouds become drops of tears over the may families and thousands of people laid off or unemployed permanently ask the same question: why? Don't we work as hard as always? We produce the same amount and the same quality product. So why are we losing our houses, our cars, our vacation and money put away for our children's education? America is silent. It is silent because it's not for the weak. Or is it that the weak ones became so strong that they simply don't care anymore? Recession, like the last mortgage payment brought to the bank, can give the sense of ownership or takes away everything. Only a miracle can direct society's attention to something other than economic problems. And the miracle happened; the war with Iraq. Everybody focused on the Persian Gulf.

- It can only happen to an idiot like me – Mark said to Andrzej sitting in his store in the morning.
- Not true. How could you foresee that the recession would unfold so fast?
- Don't try to cheer me up. I should have foreseen it. I invested everything in this store. Now I sell not per pounds but per ounces. People don't have money to spend on treats. When I talk to customers, everyone's complaining. At the end of the day I end up getting what's best so that it doesn't go bad. But how is our business?

Andrzej walked around the store. New coolers and refrigerators filled with merchandise did attract. Vegetables and fruit smelled nice laid out orderly. "What a shame" – he thought. Mark interrupted this time of reflection.

- Mister! Are you listening to me?
- Of course, sir.
- I said how was your business going?
- Honestly, I have to admit that the recession helped me. People treat money different these days; they value it and look for opportunities to get stuff cheaper. So our phones are like a dream product of recession. They sell great.
- I guess that's the only good news I've heard in a long time. Everybody's following what's going on in Iraq that they forget they don't have money to live off. I do have to do something, though. I can't just sit here and eat my products.
- Just sell this store.
- Easy to say, Andrzej. Who's gonna buy it? Everyone keeps their money tight.
- Then just shut it down and run.
- Just like that? You want me to just leave all this?
- Well, what you want to happen? You want to keep putting money in it until the cost will consume you completely? You can use your time and energy for something that will bring you some money.

- Aneta would be pissed off if she found out I dropped this damn business.
- Well, so what? It's not like you've gambled it away. You wanted what was best for her and for the kids.
- I did. I've been thinking this for days, how to ensure just the best. It came to the point where I dream about what to do the next day. I'm scared of making a mistake. What would Ania and Jasio say about the father who failed to assure them some decent future. I love them so much I'd do anything to make sure they're never short of anything.
- Slow down there. Slow down with your promises. Since when you mix money with love? Also where did this idea come from; that you have to work for your kids? Your obligation is to teach them right from wrong and everything else is left up to them. You can't take that chance from them of going through life on their own.
- And so how are they going to make it?
- Just the same way you have been. But let's better end those family practice seminars and let me get some beer. You go and get the appetizers ready. We'll go to Bogdan's and play some cards.

Bogdan's house was typical for Hamtramck; you take several steps up just to enter the living room, small room bordered with the kitchen and two other small bedrooms. On the other side of the house was a separate entrance to the apartment upstairs. The lay out of that apartment was just the same as the one's below. A small backyard with charcoal grill and the grage for two cars closed up the "Bogdan's kingdom". Friends often visited Bogdan and they liked his company. He worked for himself only, fixing cars. There was always a smile on his face and he was always willing to help. There also was no doubt that he was an expert when it came to cars. Hence, his friends called him "the man".

- So what are we playing? – Mark asked.
- Let's play "ramie".
- Sounds good – Andrzej concurred and started to give the cards away. Mark meanwhile asked "the man":
- How's business going?
- I can't complain, but the years go by and I just don't have that same energy as a while ago.
- Mine sucks – Mark didn't hide the truth – I can sell shit since people just don't have the money.
- Well, at least you've got your family with you. I've been here for fifteen yewars and still couldn't afford my wife and the kid. I always thought I just wasn't ready for it and then finally she just forgot about me and that's how our ways went in different directions. Look at me – I keep living in the same "box", fixing the same

238

cars in the same garage. This is my
life. In my free time I just go to the
bar and that's all. It would be
different in Poland.
- Different; how so?
- I'd have a purpose.
- And you can't find it here?
- No. Don't think it's a simple thing to
  find a purpose.
- The way I look at it is you should
  never feel forced to find a purpose.
  For example, I need the money
  because I don't have it. When you try
  to just quickly connect the facts you
  end up with impulsive solutions. In
  most cases this leads to making some
  careless decisions, I don't know – a
  bank robbery or something.
- What you're saying totally doesn't fit
  you – Mark commented on his
  brother's remark.
- You might be right, but as time goes
  on I start coming to different
  conclusions.
- I'm sorry to interrupt this – "the man"
  started – ut I think I've got solution to
  Mark's problems.
They looked at Bogdan with curiosity.
- What solution?
"The man" put his cards down, poured
himself a mug of beer and said:
- Buy a cab. You'll be driving alone
  and find a driver for the afternoons.
  You'll have a steady income and
  plenty of time, which you could use
  to start some new business.

239

- That's an interesting idea – Mark said.
- You'll follow in your brother's footsteps – Andrzej noted – remember how well it was going for me in Poland?
- I do, but I have to sell the store first.
- I'll help you – Andrzej with a smile – but you have to give me some space with that.
- I don't see a problem.
- Ok, you can discuss the details later, now let's get back to the cards.

Mark's children finished the grade school. In spite of the initial fear, they were doing very well. English became their everyday language and amazingly fast they were absorbing the American customs. Both Ania and Janek showed interest particularly in biology, geography and literature. Mark was happy about this – those were the subjects, which were his favorites. Besides school Ania was making her first steps towards modeling. Jane, on the other hand chose hockey. He bean playing in a youth team. Aneta was pleased to see how the kids try to spend the spare time in an organized and useful matter. Mark was helping as much as he could; drove Jasio to practices and games and Ania to fashion shows. It cost him quite a bit but never had any regrets. He was happy that the children could do all those things, often thinking about his own younger years, when sometimes he would dream about things that would never happen.

American high school differs very much from the Polish one. Kids here don't get to the same class as a group of 20 or so, for four years. Instead they switch their classes and so the teachers change frequently as well. The relationships between both the kids among themselves and between them and their teachers don't grow as strong as it would be the case in Poland. In fact the teacher-student relationship is often limited to "Hallo" and "Goodbye". Kids often don't feel comfortable in the gigantic buildings. They chose their own subjects ad each one has an individual schedule. This situation makes it impossible to get to know each other very well. Friendships are put on the back burner. Nobody really cares also to remember somebody's name.

- Where were you all night? – Mark was asking mad. Ania stood at the door with humbleness and the round circles under her eyes were the testimony that she didn't get much sleep.
- Mom and I call people, look for you in hospitals; even cops and you just stand there staring at the floor as if nothing happened.
- I went with a friend of mine.
- Nice friends you have there who drag you out for the nighttime escapades.
- You just don't understand.
- I sure don't. So why don't you explain it to me?

- She had an argument with her parents and was afraid to come back home. So we went to a park and talked the whole night.
- You couldn't bring her over here and talk all night over here?
- You'd be mad.
- And what am I like now?
- I'm sorry. It won't happen again.
- I don't want you to give me promises but to understand that that's not the way to handle things. If you cannot control your actions it means you just don't respect yourself, and if you don't respect yourself you surely can't give me the respect that I'm entitled to.
- I do understand it. I know it was dumb that's why I'm saying that it won't happen again.
- We'll see if you really understand or just think that you do. You quit the modeling classes – I said nothing. You missed a few days of school – I said nothing. Now you're not back home for the night. I still say nothing but please control yourself because you will not even know when your life will turn upside down.

Ania came up to him, hugged him and gave him a kiss on the cheek.

- Please don't be mad. I don't want you to be mad.

Mark embraced her and kissed her hair.

- The world isn't what you think it is.
  I'm not mad. I just don't want to lose
  you.

- Halo – a voice in the telephone said.
  Andrzej held it answering:
- Halo, halo.
- Is this Mr. Polskowicz.
- Speaking.
- My name s John Fresk.
- Oh, John. Did you make the decision
  yet?
- Yes, but I have a few questions – the
  voice continued.
- Go ahead.
- Why don't you want to just sell the
  store?
- It belonged to my dad – Andrzej
  started – He passed away not too long
  ago. Me, my brother and my mom
  decided to only lease it since it has a
  huge sentimental value to all of us.
- And how muc is the sentimental value
  worth?
- I don't know if I can answer this –
  Andrzej said trying to sound baffled.
- Just between you and me.
- Since you insist; seventy thousand.

The voice in the phone stopped. Andrzej felt
his heart racing. "If this works out this
would be the best deal I've ever made" – he
thought.
- Let me lose – the voice finally
  resounded on the other line.

243

- I'm not sure I understand – Andrzej said getting excited.
- I said: deal. I'll pay seventy grand.

Andrzej gave John his lawyer's phone number to assure all the details are covered. After he hang up he came up to the window humming: "After each night there comes a new day and after the storm, the quiet time…"

Mark didn't know what to say once he found out that Andrzej sold the store.
- How did you do this?
- Don't ask. What counts is that you can buy the cab and put the rest on the account towards buying a house.
- But you should get something out of it too.
- You'll do whatever you find appropriate.
- How can I return this favor to you?
- Who said you have to return something. Buy a cab and invite me for dinner.

Some see the life of a businessman to be one of luxury, one in which time goes by carelessly, one of good cars and money to spend. There is some truth to that but there is also a darker side; lies, frauds, playing games with the taxman and the law. Once someone fell into this system, stays in it for good. The initial satisfaction turns into addiction. Money no longer pleases, nor do the beautiful women or cars. We constantly look for new ways to put our skills to use. We also pay less attention to people whose problems such as family, kids, love and friendship now seem to be lame and boring. We don't care to take up creating things for others. Profit coming from every transaction takes priority over any other element of the business game. Cell phones and computers only seem to make our lives easier while in fact they are the ones to steal from us the remnants of our privacy. And so there is no more time left for a family gathering, a book, a girlfriend. The only things that matter are my business and I. And God forbid someone tries to disrupt this bottomless admiration.

Andrzej was holding on to his business. Over the course of years he got to know ways to allow him expand production. Mark drove his cab at nights and during the daytime he started overlooking some medical clinics. With time the company expanded to the extent where he could give up the taxicab driving and totally focus on the medical business. He often repeated to with gladness: "It's the first time that Americans are working for me and not the other way around". Andrzej laughing would always reply; "That's because you've found the right source of funds". And Mark would then say: "You're right. I no longer work rather I now collect the profits".
The two of them met everyday sharing the business experiences. Their spare time passed on the hockey arena where they trained the youth. Jasio still played hockey and dreamed about becoming a pro. Life was

going on day by day. Luckily the money probems were over.

- Is it that America accepted us ultimately? – Mark wondered at times.
- No – Andrzej replied – We made her accept us.

"White Star" – this was the name of the nightclub, which Konrad transformed into a discothèque style kind of place. Lit floor reminded of the one seen in "Saturday Night Life". Nice waitresses dressed in mini skirts mingled in between the tables. Peculiar music – way different than the typical American rhythms – made the place the favorite one to be visited by immigrants from Europe. Konrad used to spend a lot of time there. The "Eurotonic" people no longer absorbed him as much either. He knew Andrzej overlooked everything and so the club became his new toy.

- Well, should we have another one? – Konrad offered. The company, consisting of the Polskowicz brothers, Henio, Zbyszek, Jacek and Zdzichu, unequivocally yelled: "Pouuuur!!!" Konrad with a sense of practice opened the bottle of Smirnoff and treated the laid out glasses. Then Andrzej toasted:
- So that our children have wealthy fathers.

Everybody happily clinked their glass and throats of the connoisseurs felt strong stream of vodka. Mark began his story:

- Let me tell you what happened to me during one cab ride. One evening I got a call to pick someone up from a hotel. I drove up to the entrance and waited. After a while a young Black guy walked out. He asked me: "How much time do you have?" "All night" – I replied. He got into my cab and asked to drive him to Detroit. During the trip he told me about his family; how hard he worked to support them, etc. We stopped by one of the houses. The guy gave me fifty bucks and asked to wait for him. He came in to the house and walked out of it after a short while. Then he gave me the second address and so we went there. The same thing; he gives me fifty bucks, goes to the house, walks out of it. And so we drive for about four hours. Around 3 am he brought with him a black girl. The two of them told me to take them here and there. She must have been a prostitute because every time she walked out from a house she just looked awful. Finally the two of them had an argument and he asked me to stop. Once I stopped he grabbed her by her hair and threw her out of the car. She yelled something but I didn't even care anymore to wait I pushed the gas and drove off. "How much do I owe you?" – he asked. I said: "You gave me a hundred. Give me anther hundred and we'll be cool".

247

The guy reached to his pocket and I turning reached my hand out to get my money from him. At this moment instead of the money in his hand, I saw a gun. He put it against my head and said: "We'll do this; you give me back the hundred I gave you. Add to it another hundred and then we'll be cool." I didn't know what to do. That son of a bitch wanted to rob me, not only that, he also played with me all along. I was so angry I wanted to choke him with bare hands. But he had a gun.

Everybody listened in suspense. Zbyszek kept asking: "And? And?"

- I took the keys out of the ignition, walked out of the car and started to walk along the street. "Stop or I'll shoot!" – the dude yelled. But I didn't care. I was not going to give him a penny; I thought to myself and kept marching. At some point I stopped and turned around looking to see where my attacker was. Nobody... I thought he ran without even being able to react in any way. Only after some time, when I thought about this whole situation I came to conclusion that it was not the smartest thing to do on my part. I should have given him the money and not take chances.

- Well, you don't know what would happen had you given him the money either – Konrad said.

248

- Maybe you're right. Anyway, since that time I put a bulletproof window inside my cab. I had never used it before.

Konrad opened another bottle and poured the liquor to the glass.

- Maybe that's enough – Andrzej said – We'll get wasted like puppies.
- Come on, we're just beginning to drink.
- You know it's interesting thing with the whole drinking issue. – Henio. - Once I had a partner with whom we opened a gas station. It was tough at the beginning. We had to get the business rolling and get the whole paperwork figured out. We worked ten, sometimes twelve hours a day. Finally things got on the right track; the money started to flow like river and we were even able to hire two additional people to take care of the administrative stuff. This is when my partner met that girl. Well, he had known her from their high school years. She was a bit older than him. His parents constantly tried to talk him out of her but she was the focus of his life. After some time they moved in together. His friends told him: "Leave her. She's not worthy". But he never listened and loved her to death. They stopped coming to the parties or visiting anyone. She was the sole center of his life and love took away his ability to think

reasonably. He forgot the facts and was unable to carry on a normal conversation.

- Who was that girl? – Mark asked.

Henio, with mysterious smile, answered;

- Clear and pure, and her name was Vodka.

Everybody looked at each other yet nobody laughed.

- There's a lot of truth to what you've just said. – Andrzej. – I myself knew plenty of guys who died in all kinds of car crashes driving drunk. Just take a look at the homeless; half of them have degrees and the booze ruined them completely.
- All right, all right. You guys stop talking about this booze, 'cause you're just taking away my appetite. – Konrad.
- OK then, let's drink to the life that's wise. – Mark proposed the toast and everybody clinked repeating after him: - To wise life!

Mark pulled u at the driveway. The garage door opened automatically and the white jeep drove in. The house was absolutely gorgeous, large... the marble floors shined and tall windows gave the greatest view of the park. Mark caught up with America. He was satisfied and happy that he could provide for his family, which had been his dream for so long. Indeed, he enjoyed walking around the house, of which value now was around four hundred thousand. His car was luxurious and modern class. The medical company was perfectly stable. You could say: what a life. But deep inside there was something that bothered him and did not let him enjoy all this to the fullest. He thought about it for hours. The answer was very simple, so simple it was hard to accept it. He simply was unable to admit that fear constantly kept complicating his life. It was just the ordinary fear of losing it all. He'd think: "Why kids aren't doing so good in school anymore? The more I invest in them the less they think about studies. They could care less about books. Music they listen to is nothing but garbage. The way they talk is far away from an intelligent and rational form of discussion. They consider my views to be silly and old-fashioned. Well, maybe they're right; I did grow old".

- What are you thinking about? – Aneta asked.
- About the kids. You know, I asked tem to read some Sienkiewicz or "War and Peace". It's been two years and they haven't even started yet.
- Well, get ready for this. – Aneta. – The school called in the morning. Ania was caught smoking pot.
- What? Where is she now?
- In jail.

The boat rocked on the water smooth and peaceful. After the years of struggle in the business world, Andrzej was finally able to afford a new toy. Long with leather interior, the boat ended with a cozy cabin and was empowered by a large motor. It wasn't top of the line luxury boat but for Andrzej it was enough and – what's more important – it allowed him to just get away from the daily routine of constant running and catching up with everything. So he would sit on his boat looking ahead, all the way to the horizon of the lake Michigan. The beautiful colors of water made him sometime feel as if it were warm ocean waters. He rode it a little farther to the end of the peninsula, which protected the gulf from strong waves and winds. The electronic devices on the boat showed the depth of two hundred meters. "Amazing, I never thought it could get this deep", he thought. He sailed it even further towards the open lake. The wind got stronger and at some point Andrzej no longer felt comfortable. Waves crashed against the boat with double strength. Andrzej kept sailing. Blue sky and the rays of sun were the promise of the beautiful weather that day. But the waves and wind seemed to be saying something quite opposite. His boat no longer rocked peacefully on the wave, of which size kept growing every minute. "You don't scare me – he talked to himself – I went through more scary times I life. Wind is nothing to me".

He held on to the wheel strongly and at the same time kept going faster. By now it reached some hundred miles per hour jumping in the air with every larger wave that crashed against it. "Yes! Higher! Higher!" – Andrzej screamed. The contours of the peninsula disappeared behind his back and he was now on the open lake, far away from the shore. He reached to his bag to get a tape. Another high wave hit the front of the boat. Andrzej lost balance and fell. Once the boat dropped back on the water he picked up the tape and quickly inserted into the player. Pleasant music began to resound from the speakers. As he looked around the shoreline disappeared completely. "Time to go back", he though. The sun hid behind clouds and the water changed its color to black. Powerful waves with huge white foam hit the boat with double frequency. He turned around looking at his compass; "East – that's right". He headed towards the shore. With surprise he noticed that waves that so far were torturing his boat from the front now changed direction. Instead of supporting his effort to go towards the shore, they began to attack him from the front again. Heavy drops of rain it the boat. "What a weather. Everything changed in the matter of seconds", he thought. The temperature dropped so much that Andrzej had to put a warm winter coat on. The storm raged with full strength. The visibility was zero. He spoke to himself: "Is somebody just playing with me now. Nothing like vacationing by the Baltic. Friends, girls and it never took us to wide waters". He looked ahead ut the visibility continued to be none. His hands were freezing and he had difficulty steering the boat. Wind grew so strong that Andrzej no longer could breath easily. "Just twenty more minutes and I'll be by the shore". He looked ahead and this time froze: a wall of

water suddenly stood right in front of him.
He grabbed the wheel as strongly as he could.
The tall wave lifted up the boat just to
momentarily drop it into the black abbeys of
water. Crack, sound of broken glass and
wood was overpowered by the wind.
Nobody could also hear his voice, or perhaps
he didn't even scream…

- How many times did I tell you to stay
  away from drugs?! – Mark.

Ania looked at him agitated and kept quiet.

- Now you see how it is. You went to
  court, the judge said you smoked pot
  and there was no discussion.
- It wasn't mine.
- Why are you even saying this? You
  know it makes no difference whose
  stash it was. You smoked it and
  that's what counts.
- I don't want to spend here six months
  – she started to sound dramatic.
- Be glad you're in the juvenile and not
  in the real prison.
- Will you help me to get out of here?
- I'll see what I can do. Remember in
  the future that what I once said really
  is true; you make a decision – be
  ready for the consequences. And
  don't expect me to fix your mistakes.
  If you get used to it you'll be like a
  handicapped for life.
- I know, but everything in life turns
  the other way than it was meant.
- That's why some people do great
  while others are starving. There are

no secrets in life. All you have to do
is be who you are, who you really are.
Look at you – you are a beautiful
blond with gorgeous long hair and
shining blue eyes. Looking at you is
like listening to a romantic melody
under beautiful sunny sky. This is
your true, natural look. Now think
how much time and energy you spend
just trying to destroy this beautiful
image. Rap, cigarettes, drugs, booze
and boys, who can't even think
straight. It just doesn't suit you so
don't try to force yourself to be
somebody you're not.

Ania listened to it realizing that never before
did she identify her beauty with her habits or
behavior. She did start to notice the
similarities and differences alike. "Who am
I, really?" – she thought. Her dad interrupted
the reflection.

- Here's a book for you to read. It's
  my favorite, "Quo Vadis". I really
  would love for you to read it. And
  don't tell me you don't have time for
  this now – he finished smiling. Ania
  smiled back to him and embraced
  saying:
- Will you visit me often?
- Of course will. You'll get to see me
  more often than at home.

Ania didn't know what to say. "Maybe dad
is right. Maybe I do send too much time
away from home..." The visitation time was
over and the guard let him know that it was

time to go. Ania waived goodbye and
walked away down the hallway.
"Maybe it'll be for the best", he thought.
After visiting Ania, Mark went home. He
walked into the kitchen and saw Aneta
crying.

- Don't tell me something else
  happened. I've had enough for today,
  especially after going to the juvenile.

Aneta walked up to him and handed a letter
from the police of Traverse City. Mark sat
down and started to read.
"Dear Mr. Polskowicz,
It is with sadness that we have to inform you
that a boat Bay Liner" was found near
Traverse City. The numerals on the boat
indicate that it belonged to your brother,
Andrzej. The investigation report says that
your brother sailed on the lake Michigan
alone, on June 26, 1999, at 10 am. We can
only suspect that at some point he was
surprised by a sudden storm sometime
around 11 am. In spite of the very intense
rescue and search operation, which lasted
three days, we were unfortunately unable to
find your borther's body. The investigation
is at this point complete and all
circumstances point out to the tragic
drowning of your brother. Please accept our
sincere condolences.
Signed: Traverse City Police Chief.

Chapter V

After many years of intense training and hundreds of miles gone from one game to another, Janek's hockey team began to shape up. He got on his high school team as a forward. Mark was very happy to hear the news. Overall this was also his success. He took his son to practices, helped organizing meets and tournaments. He really wanted Janek to absorb the qualities such as discipline and self determination, which in the future would help him achieving whatever the goals

- Congratulations – Mark said.
- Thank you. – Janek. – But it's a shame that we won't be driving together anymore.
- Don't worry. I'll still be coming to your games. You're in high school now and it's time to start taking care of your own self.
- I don't see any problems. You'll see it'll be all right.
- I know. And those years we spent on ice – they weren't in veins. I'm proud of you, really. You'll see what joy can come from making your own decisions now.
- Sometimes joy, and sometimes regret.
- What makes you think that?
- I know some friends who were good in athletics but once their fathers kind of stepped away, their sport careers ended.

- Well, see? It all makes sense only
  when both father and son share the
  same goal. This is why I never
  wanted you to pursue my dreams and
  I think it worked.
- I think so too, dad. I like this sport
  and I like this lifestyle.
- Hence I have a surprise for you.
- Wow! What surprise?
- I got you a car.

Janek's eyes shined with excitement.
- What kind?
- S-10 Chevy.
- This is great! Dad, you're the best!
- Just remember, this is not a reward
  for something, but a form of support
  for you to get closer to your goals.

Father's love doesn't shine like a diamond in
a golden band. It more reminds of coal, to
which to get. We go through tons of soil,
dust and danger but once we get to the
treasure we look at the black stone with
humbleness. With time we also realize that
even a small sparkle can light this solid stone.
The redness it acquires once burning, the
spurs of flames it produces tell us that we
achieved what we had worked for so hard;
the father's love. So, let's look for this
sparkle, the sparkle which can put so much
life in this – seemingly useless and dead
stone.

- Why has Janek skipped so many days
  of school? – Aneta asked.

- Why are you asking me about this? –
  Mark.
- You could get a little more involved.
- I do what I can. Besides, he is
  already old enough to know right
  from wrong.
- They kicked him out of the team and
  it's because of all those missed school
  days.
- I was afraid it would end like this.
- Well, then do something.
- It's his turn now. But it seems like he
  kind of followed my way. Once he
  got the free hand the school stopped
  being important, so did the hockey
  and soon we won't be important
  either.
- No, it's not going to happen. He
  loves us.
- Maybe he does, but with his love not
  ours. He thinks we exist to always
  support him and he should be the
  focus of everything we do. He can't
  find the spark.
- What spark?
- The spark of understanding.
- What are you talking about? All kids
  are the same.
- You're right, there are only few who
  can come to the right conclusion.
- So what are we going to do?
- Let's wait for Jasio to come to the
  right conclusions.
- And what if he doesn't?

Mark didn't answer. Deep in his heart he felt hurt by his son for losing so quickly what they both worked on for so long.

Lifestyle of the American youth differs significantly from what we would call a normal life. Billboards and advertisements dictate what to wear, what to talk about, what music to listen to and how to behave. Everything got so commercialized; the youth are pretty much left with no choices. But there is a thing that remained intact. It has lasted for years and always has been the best protection against the crazy propaganda of current civilization. It's called common sense and rational thinking. It's not easy to define one's own self. It also takes time to choose the right way of life and to acquire the right habits. But as the reward, we could say we get the real us, as opposed to product of imagination.

Janek allowed to be sucked in into the world that isn't real. What do you call a toll blond, blue-eyed young man born in Poland now wearing baggy jeans dropped almost to the knees? Is the rap music that talks about life in gangs filled with drugs and alcohol be a part of his life? How much work and self-determination it must take for a young man to actually star believing that he is someone he's never been? To try to convince him that he is talented and smart, and that there is great future waiting for him, means to make him angry.

What is so magical about our life? In a second we are able to believe that we're on the bottom of the barrel. Faith in one's own value and dignity disappears just as fast. Laziness? This seems to be the only reasonable answer. Why work and train own self so that in the future there is a person to be proud of? In the big and colorful world there are heroes waiting for us too. We can start imitating and identifying with them very quickly. For just ten bucks we can buy a CD that ill tell us how to live and what to wear. But we refuse to accept that our life will be worthy just as much as the initial investment.

A group of friends came to visit Mark and Aneta. They all sat comfortably in armchairs and drank beer. Ania came back from the juvenile and told everybody about her experiences. Janek was listening to her stories and with a smile commented on particular events.
Mark discussed with his friend Zbyszek about president Clinton's sex adventures. Women talked about every day issues at work and at home. At some point Janek announced:
- I'd like to say something.
- What is it? – Mark.
- 'd like to say that I'm changing schools.
The room got quiet and even Ania looked at her brother with disbelief.
- Teachers don't like me. They constantly look for a hole in the whole.
- And you think that it will be better in new school? – Mark.

262

- Of course.
- Give the kid a chance. – Zbyszek.
- It's not up to us. – Mark. His school – his chance. I've told him long time ago to stop hanging out with that crowd; booze, cigarettes, staying up till morning. How can you even function?
- I neither drink nor smoke. But I will change school anyway.
- Times change. – Zbyszek's wife.
- Kids would just like to get everything within one year nowadays. – Aneta.
- Maybe that's good if they want to get on their own feet fast. – Zbyszek.
- Well, I disagree. – Mark. – They can't have everything right away because they'll lose meaning in life. If you want to get by own your own, fine, but you have to know laws and regulations. It's only then that you can really get around them.
- What about the car? – Zbyszek's wife.
- What car? – Mark asked puzzled.
- Janek promised me that he would seriously go back to his studies and hockey practice, but he asked me to tell you. –
- Tell me what? – Mark was even more surprised now.
- Well, before you came we talked about the car. Janek complains that he doesn't have much room for the hockey equipment. Besides, it's only two people car and sometimes he

263

drives with his friends and needs more space. So, he asked us to convince you to sell his car and get him a larger one.

Mark kept sitting in silence. "Where are the limits of my patience and how long will I tolerate all this?   The most reasonable thing to do would be to bring everyone's peace of mind back by simply saying 'no'. What they're asking me to do is so against my rules. On the other hand I do love my son and want his life to be easier than mine".

Ania interrupted his thinking.

- Get him another car, dad. Please, he could take me to school. – She said with the voice that broke Mark's any objections. After a moment he asked his wife:

- What do you think about it?

- Get a new one. He doesn't like the car he has now.

"Well, that's something new – he thought – since when a sixteen year old can like or dislike the car that was a gift?"

- Don't think too much. – Zbyszek. – Get him that car. You'll see, he'll shape up.

- Yes, definitely he will. – They were talking one over another.

- All right. We'll get another car but this time you can't disappoint me. – Mark finally decided.

- Dad, everything we'll be ok. Thank you so very much for changing this car for me.

Mark knew he made a mistake. Their paths take different courses very quickly and nothing can change it. Years of teaching the basic things such as reading or writing, biking, swimming – they seemed to simple now. Now, after all these years Mark realized that his authority diminished t the point where feelings just don't count. Now it's the game time, where people simply make it look like they love and want to be loved. In fact, however, the kids want to test how far they can push it with their parents. The saddest part of this game is that we allow them to win.

- Mr. Polskowicz, – A man in suit and eye-burning red tie said – You really insist on buying this arena? – Mark looked at the bank president with a smile.
- I sure do. I wouldn't be here otherwise.
- This is, however, a very unusual situation. You want to borrow 1.5 million and we don't know if you have enough experience to run this hockey arena.
- I did send you evidence that I own a company that runs medical clinics. I do, therefore, have experience in management.
- I know, and I do have to admit that your portfolio is impressive. Bu medical is something different than a hockey arena. We have to decline your loan application.

265

Mark was looking at the man with mixed feelings. "For what did I tell him about that medical business of mine. Now the fat bastard screwed me over. Janek would be so happy if I bought this arena. We could work together like in good old times".

- Would you like to say or add something, sir? – The bank president. Mark "woke up", gathered his thoughts and after a while said:
- My medical business brings me enough profit to feel and live comfortably, as you well know. But, there is something that you don't know about.

Fat man looked at him with curiosity waiting for continuation.

- Long time ago, in Poland, I was one of the best hockey players in the league. My father was elected the President of the Polish Hockey League for the northern Poland. Well, he didn't have much time for hockey because at the same time he was a CEO in paper manufacturing company. So he basically gave me the whole paper work hockey-related. I was in charge of organizing the league, in chare of equipment, organizing tournaments, etc. In 1983 I had elbow injury and could not later come back to the team. Now, I've fallen in love with this sport so much that I decided to dedicate my life to it. The situation, however, forced me to move out of the country. Now, after

266

many years, being a respected citizen that I am, I'd like to go back to what has been my dream for so long. Therefore, I think that just running a hockey arena is a piece of cake compared to what I was responsible for in Poland.

Mark stopped and looked at the president who wiped the sweat off of his forehead.

- I didn't know anything about your past, but I now understand why you want to take up this field. That's a very interesting biography you have here. Congratulations.
- Well, what is the situation with respect to my loan now?
- I can't give you an answer now. – Fat man stood up. – But I can assure you that I will give your application my personal recommendation at the nearest meeting.
- Does it mean that I have good chances to get that loan?
- If I give you my personal recommendation, you can feel the owner of that arena.

Mark shook his hand and walked out to the hallway.

"See, my brother. I've learnt to pull some lies too. You'd be proud". – He thought.

He was driving down the street in a silver sport car. He really was pleased to have convinced the banker. "Sometimes a lie is the necessity – he thought – to be able to get to the goal. Andrzej was a master of it. I am probably just as talented but never practiced", he smiled.

The street he took was in the northern part of metro Detroit. It reached from lake saint Clair through middle class neighborhoods, through the mall and finally got to the city of Bloomfield, one of the wealthiest in the United States. He liked that route. It reminded him the history of his American career; from poverty through advancement to the middle class, to even higher shelf. Large houses and neatly mowed grass were the indicators that he was approaching Bloomfield. He sped up a bit and turned the volume of his radio up. He was in excellent mood.

"Once I buy that arena, I'll have two companies. Kids will grow out of this temporary stupidity. When they finished schooling they'll take over my business and I'll be enjoying golf". His daydreaming was interrupted by the sound of his cell phone.

- Halo? – Mark.
- Is this Mr. Polskowicz?
- Speaking.
- This is special agent Johnson with the FBI.

Mark was totally shocked.

- I have a question to you regarding your brother.
- I have to disappoint you, but my brother is dead. He died a year ago on lake Michigan.
- This is why I'm calling you. In spite of some very intense search operation his body has never been found, which

is rather unusual. We looked into the history of your brother's life and we know that at some point you both lived in Hollywood.   Is that correct?

- Yes it is, but does it have to do with anything?
- For how long had you known a girl named Angela?
- Four months, maybe five, but…

The agent wouldn't let him finish.

- Well, I have to tell you something. At the same time when Angela died, there was an earthquake in L.A., correct?
- That's right.
- During this earthquake an alarm went off in one of the banks in the area. The police dispatched a patrol car but they saw nothing. They didn't really take a good look at the situation thinking probably that the alarm was activated by the earthquake. Well, the next day it turned out that somebody wiped out the cash completely.

Mark started to laugh and said:

- What do we have to do with any of this? We have an alibi; the four of us were in our apartment.
- Please don't interrupt me. – The voice on the other side got very serious. – We reviewed the surveillance tape from the bank. It shows that at the moment of the earthquake a man broke into the bank and walked out with the money. He left the bag in a

garbage can on the parking lot in front of it. Then he walked away to unknown destination. A few minutes after a VW drove to the parking lot and a woman walked out of it. Her image matches Angela. She took the bag and drove away.

- I still don't see a connection. – Mark.
- Please, listen. That same VW was in an accident half an hour after leaving the bank parking lot. We calculated that it takes seven to ten minutes to get from the bank to the scene of the accident. Where was she for the twenty unaccounted minutes? The accident was professionally staged; burnt face, hands – they weren't even examined during the autopsy. We decided to exhume the body and it turned out that the girl who died in that accident was not Angela.
- Who, then? – Mark yelled curious?
- This is irrelevant. What is the most puzzling...

Mark couldn't continue like this. Thoughts began to spin and his hand started to shake.

- Could you stop for a sec? I have to pull over somewhere. I can't drive anymore now.

He took a side street and parked on the shoulder.

- Ok, go on now.
- So, we checked her address... - The agent started again.
- That's right! – Mark. – Her father lives there!

270

- It was not her father. We couldn't find him. But what's most interesting is that the house where she lived, was bought by a Polish immigrant woman, whose sketch matched that of Angela.
- That's impossible! She didn't speak Polish and spoke with typical American accent.
- That doesn't matter. These are the facts.

Mark got quiet trying to get all those facts in order. "Polish woman – that's impossible. I would have figured it out".

- Halo, are you still there? – The agent.
- Yes, I am. But what does my brother have to do with any of this?
- We don't have basis to accuse your brother of anything but his acquaintanceship with that woman is thought provoking.
- So why are you calling me?
- Honestly, I just wanted to ask you one question.
- What is it?
- Have you met that woman in the past, in Poland?
- I've already told you that I would never even think she might be Polish.
- Ok, please don't get upset. I was just asking.
- I'm not getting upset but you're implying that my brother didn't die, so he is alive somewhere.
- I did not say that but just in case, for future reference please take my number down.

- In what case? - Mark started to get mad.
- In case you, for example, want to know what time is it.

Mark laughed.

- I do have to give it to you; as for an agent you do have a sense of humor.
- I'm trying my best and I thank you sincerely for your time.
- Hold on yet. Could you tell me the real name of the girl?
- Yes, but it won't be easy for me to pronounce.

The agent began to spell "Ka-tar-zi-na"...

- Katarzyna? – Mark. - What about the last name?
- Pitar. – Johnson, quickly this time. Mark wrote down the name and thanked.
- Thank you, agent Johnson. You gave me some hope here.
- Please don't take it out of proportions. These are just our indications.

Mark hang up. "Could this be true? Andrzej would not hide this from me".

Champagne corks were popping one after another. Guests invited were of various professions; doctors, lawyers, constructors, factory workers. All of them were now united by one hobby: hockey. After the mane bureaucratic barriers and submission of hundred of documents Mark opened up his own hockey arena.

There are times in life when satisfied with our work we want to put what we've learned to use. Mark's financial condition allowed that and so with great joy he watched the first game played on his own hockey arena. Even though the whole object required renovation and some necessary repairs, the locker rooms and ice were ready for the players.

Now how often does it happen that young generation wants to work together hand in hand with the older? But in this case everyone was on the same page: "our arena, our problem, our games". Everybody was eager to help starting with the sixty years olds and with some barely walking yet three year olds on the other end. Hockey is so popular in Michigan that entire families participate in the league structure. High ranking of the Detroit Red Wings motivate and inspire the next adepts of this challenging sport.

Mark was standing in front of the large glass window, in the restaurant through which he could watch what was happening on ice. Sometimes someone would come up to him to congratulate. People would say:

- This is exactly what we needed in our neighborhood. You really did a favor not only for the kids but also for the older ones.

"It won't be too profitable of the business but it's a joy to do something for others". – Mark thought.

Janek interrupted his reflections.

- This is a bomb.
- I'm glad you like it.
- Can I work here?

- Of course. You are my son.
  Everything you see here, I did for
  you.
- And I'll be able to teach the kids to
  skate? – Janek was really excited.
- Yup. This is the basic for the future
  of hockey, isn't it? Some day, when
  you finish studies, you'll be able to
  organize an amateur league and
  tournaments. For now just make sure
  that the locker rooms are clean after
  games and check the measurers on the
  compressor.
- Ok, dad. I'll take care of everything.
  You can go home.
- Yes, boss. – Mark with a smile.

The yacht club was located right at the feet of
the ocean. Wide staircase covered with red
carpet led to the second floor and to the
restaurant. Bar was decorated with shark
teeth and reminded of a large cabin. Dimmed
lights and gentle jazz music provided the
place with cozy atmosphere. Table in the
corner was by the window with the view over
the ocean. It was taken by two people; a
woman in her thirties, dressed in black and
brown costume. Stylish gold necklace
around her neck accentuated the subtle
OBOJCZYK. Her breasts, like oranges filled
with life giving nectar, were perfectly
synchronized with the rest of her body. Her
hair, blonde, cut very short, suggested that
the woman had a charming yet firm
personality. The man who accompanied her
was dressed very elegantly and had to be

around forty years of age. Dark suit, right shirt with burgundy tie and on his hand shined a gold watch. His hands were delicate and well cared for. It was easy to see that he belonged to the wealthy people. A server approached their table.

- Can I get you a beverage?
- Spanish coffee please. – The woman.
- And for you, sir?
- I'd like a glass of wine, Italian and from the south. If you have one from Naples or Latina, that would be perfect.
- What year would you prefer, sir?
- 1985. – The man without thinking much. The waiter walked away and the man looked intensely in the green eyes of the woman. They shined in the light of the candles. After a moment he said:
- Well, but let me finish that story I started to tell you. So, one guy wanted to make business by selling shoes from U.S. to Russia. He went to the Russians to show them what he had to offer. Once they saw the product they were at aw. "Please sell us the ones you're showing now" – they said. But he didn't want to. "Why?" – the Russian asked. "Because I only brought one shoe of each promo pair". "Where is the rest of the shoes?" – they kept asking him. "They are in the U.S.". "Do you need to go to a psychiatrist?" – the Russians were puzzled. "No, why?".

The man stopped with his story and looked at the woman laughing.

- I so much enjoy seeing you smile like this. You don't know what joy it is to me.
- I always laugh at your incredible stories. No one can pull lies like you.
- Sometimes I lie for fun and sometimes out of the necessity.
- I know, this is why I love you so much. And I do have to say it – you are the master of it. They way you handled the passports issue in L.A.; nobody could do it better.
- Thank you, but it's you who inspires my actions.

The server brought the drinks and walked away again.

- Well, let's drink to our life. – The woman offered. – Let's drink to only lying for fun.
- To sweet lies. – Andrzej concurred.

They drank up.

- It never occurred to me that I could be so happy here in Argentina. – The man started again.
- And what am I supposed to say? I've always wanted to be a flight attendant and travel the world. Now I'm sitting here with you sipping exclusive cocktail. The truth of the matter is though; it doesn't really matter where I live as long as you're near me.
- Great love, great risk. We've come a long way already; the dangers, parting, arguments and goodbyes.

Yet, we're still together. I love you and I want you to always remember about it.

- Come on, let's go home. I want to feel you inside of me. I want you to make love to me. When you kiss my breasts and caress my body, I am waiting inside for you. I know I want you now, right now.

Her shining eyes were glued to the man. He took her by the hand and kissed it.

- You know you've always been and always will be my best lover. Maybe a day will come that you'll give birth to my son.

Their conversation was interrupted by a guy sitting at the next table.

- I terribly apologize, but I couldn't stop myself. You speak with such beautiful accent I just had to ask where do you come from?

The woman opened her mouth to say something but at the same time the man accompanying her said:

- Let me answer. Please, don't get me wrong, sir. I work for the government and unfortunately I can't tell you what country I represent. I can give you a little bit of a hint if you promise that it'll stay between us.

The man was looking with signs o obvious surprise on his face not knowing what to say. One could tell by the look on his face that he regretted ever starting this conversation. The man meanwhile continued:

- II will just say that I was the major link to the end of the Falkland war.

The stranger looked at him respectfully.

- I'm not going to ask anything else. – He said and walked away.

The woman laughed so hard she started to cry.

- I love you, you liar, I love you.
- You still want to go home?
- I want you now even more.

The man grabbed her hand. The two of them stood up and left.

The situation looked good. Like it was expected many teams decided to rent the arena for their practices and games. Paying the loan off was not a problem. Mark and Jasio ran their own skating school and in the free time participated in tournaments. Mark was the coach and Jasio the main forward. The relation father-son resembled idealistic fairytales. In case situation however, it was reality.

This evening their team played the final game of the tournament. Mark nervously walked among the players encouraging them.

- We have five minutes left. It's a tie now. Worse case scenario we'll go to the overtime.
- Chill, coach. Whatever will be – will be. – One of the players replied.
- No, we can't think like that. I have a plan that will get us win in this game.
- Well, let's get on it. Time is running out.

- Ok, listen. Here's what we're going to do. Their third five looks tired. We'll get our first five on ice against their third and we'll pull one defender to add anther midfielder.
- Which one?
- Janek.
- That will work.

Mark walked up to his son.
- They will block their defense. You still the puck and go straight for the goal. Don't give up just go straight towards the net and shoot.
- Easy to say.
- Never in my life have I won a cup yet. Now is the chance and you can help making my dream come true.

Janek didn't answer. The time came for the teams to conduct the changes. Janek jumped over the band and skated to where the game was about to be restarted. Mark looked at his watch. "Only one minute" – he thought. The referee dropped the puck between the two players and Mark's tem rushed right away to block their counterparts. The puck was in the middle of the ice. Janek freed himself from the opponent sped up starting at the blue line and stole the puck. The audience was on its feet and Mark clinched his fists. Janek skated incredibly fast and the road to the net was right in front of him. Mark looked at the watch again. Only ten seconds left.
- Now! Shoot! – Mark screamed. Janek was very close now but didn't fire only tackled the goalie making him totally disorientated. The goalie leaned in different direction,

279

which is when Janek with great precision placed the puck in the net.

"Gooooaaaal!" - the whole audience screamed and so did Mark. The entire team rushed to congratulate Janek. After the game there was the official ceremony of handing the cup. The speaker announced:

- And the winning team is The Summit Lightnings! The cup is being received by the team captain, John Polskowicz. Congratulations to the coach, Mark Polskowicz.

Applause on the audience and the cheers of the young people made Mark feel great. At the end Janek handed thee cup to his father. Mark lifted it above his head and held until the parents of team players were done taking pictures. "This is the son I wanted. More important, this is the son I have", he thought. Once the area emptied out Mark walked around thinking. Then the doors opened and a man walked in. Right away Mark recognized a member of the city's housing commission.

- Good evening, Mr. Polskowicz.
- How are you? What can I do for you this late hour?
- I have some badnews for you.

The good mood Mark was in, disappeared instantly. He didn't know how to react. "Am I going to enjoy life once a year now, or what?", he thought. The official didn't wait for Mark to start asking questions. He sat on the bench and looking at ice began to talk.

- I have a lot off respect and admiration for your creativity and ambition. But during the last council meeting a decision was made to close the arena until the renovation is over. Besides the plans of expansion and remodeling do not meet the guidelines and will have to be adjusted.

- Well, this would mean additional costs.
- I know, but that's the law.
- Fuck the law. You want me to put handicapped accessible restrooms in locker rooms for the hockey players. You tell me to put water sprinkles over the ice. What kind of nonsense is that? This would cost me some seven hundred thousand.
- I understand your position, but this is official decision and there is nothing I can do.
- In that case I can do nothing but sell this thing. Maybe someone will build a supermarket here or something. That would be a trill for the kids, wouldn't it? – Mark talked ironically now. The man walked up to him trying to shake his hand for goodbye. Mark refused. Instead he turned back saying:
- You represent retarded law and you know it. I want nothing to do with people like that.

Two weeks after this conversation the hockey arena was closed and put up for sale. Mark sat in his office when his wife called.

- Guess what happened.

- Tell me. Nothing can surprise me these days anymore.
- Janek stole two of your checks and tried to cash them. They figured it out at the bank right away and called the cops. Of course he's in jail now.
- I'll call you later. – Mark hang up.

"Is living on this earth supposed to be some kind of a punishment for me? Animals have better life than humans. They teach their little ones to walk, show them how to get food and then do as you wish. We put all this time and energy in dumb heads. We kiss, e care, we teach good from bad and at the end we get a big fat kick in the ass. We dream about love and family just so that at the end we can come to conclusion that the best years we had were those of being bachelors. Then we were treated like people. Now that we're married we have to take up the role of servers. We just take orders from members of the family and get punished if we are later with the delivery".

Thoughts like this span through Mark's head. "First, the daughter and her fiends who had nothing else to offer than drugs. Then, the son who as the thank you for dropping out of school got a new car. Now, maybe in the moment of passion and maybe because he wanted to thank me, he steals my money. Why a house for four hundred thousand? Why the new cars? The more I invest in family the stronger barriers between us arise. And what about me? I try as hard as I can to make this brutal life easier on all of them. Mornings go by on trying to solve problems at work and evenings on trying to solve problems at home".

"What about me?" – the question resounded in his mind. I've always thought that good should be rewarded with good. I don't even have time anymore for love, the beautiful love I enjoyed so much when I was younger. The delicate kisses, talks for hours in the evening walks and the scent in the air – where has all this gone?"

The judge looked at Mark with sympathy.

- After your daughter's case I didn't think I would see you here again, sir.
- I didn't expect this either.
- What got to you to steal your father's money? – the judge addresses Janek now.
- I only wanted to borrow. – He replied.
- Has your father ever refused helping you financially?
- No, never.
- Please take that car away from him. – The judge now said to Mark who nodded in accordance.
- I can either lock him up for a few months so that he get a grip, or you can pay the fines and we'll let him go.

Aneta insisted that he pays the fines. Initially Mark wasn't up for this.

"Maybe if he goes to jail for a while it would wake him up" – he deliberated within himself but she insisted:

- Come one. He's going to become a wreck if he goes there.

Mark didn't feel like talking much about this anymore. He paid the fines.

A man was lying on the sun bed looking at the surface of the lake right by his house. Greens surrounded the palm trees, around which colorful birds were making their rounds.

"What a beautiful day. It just screams "Create something to match this great scenario"" – He thought. He reached out for his guitar nearby. Pleasant sounds began to travel through the veranda. On the opposite side, by the entrance to the garage, a woman was washing a car. Her energetic and confident movements suggested she found joy in the activity.

- What are you doing out there? – She yelled towards the man.
- Playing a guitar.
- You could help me, you know?
- You know so well I can't. That's what the sponges and brushes are for.
- Oh, of course. I forgot it is against your convictions to wash your own car.
- Don't throw my convictions in it. Washing the car can be a very dangerous thing to do. You can sprang your wrist or something, or…
- All right, all right. Don't start with you deliberations on this subject. Better start playing something nice. Once I'm done I'll sit down with you and listen.

The man gently played the strings and soon started to sing:
"Once I saw you the first time, I started to live again like a flower touched by the sun. The storm in the sky won't scare me, for I'll always keep you in my memory. Do you believe in God beyond the clouds? He is the master of our lives. But if you don't want to believe this, the at least give me your hand and live these moments with me".
The woman came close and sat next to him.

- Maybe you're right. It's probably better that you sing then wash cars.

The man stopped playing. He sipped a bit from his glass and said:

- Tell me your whole story, please. I only know the pieces and it bothers me.

The woman moved around in her chair with the feeling of uneasiness. She lit up a cigarette and said:

- We've lived here in Buenos Aires for quite a few years now. I've never thought that Argentina can resemble Poland to me. Such a huge country and only 32 million people. The great pampa, where the cowboys live, the "gauchos" silver lakes and rivers running curly towards the ocean.
- Argentina in Spanish, and in Latin, means SREBORZE. But why are you telling me about Argentina? I asked you to tell me the story of your life.
- I don't know. It just came up. Buenos resembles to me Gdansk, Pampa, Pomerania. Thirty two

285

million people is close to the numbers of Poland.

- Just that Poland's territory is much smaller. – The man added with a smile.
- Stop it. Don't laugh at me.
- All right, al right. I'll stop.
- Besides, you know already the story of my life. I told you so many times. You know whom I've slept with and with whom I've argued, where I went to school and what my dreams were.
- But I don't understand one thing. Why did you rob that bank?
- Ok, since you so insist I'll tell you. I met a guy in Poland. His name was George. He promised me all these golden hills, said he'd marry me etc. So I come to America. With time memories were everything that was left after all those promises. He treated me like an object, wasn't giving me any money, everything he made he'd hide. I made some extra money working as a waitress. One day he talked me into buying shares in one of the banks. I gave him the money. Later on it turned out that the bank was owned by one of George's friends. Everything they made they split between them and those who bought their shares were left with nothing. I promised myself not to let it go that easy. I met this guy who played pool with you in L.A. He wrote music for movies and has been

around in the Hollywood world. One day the action of the movie was taking place in that very bank. In the midst of everything that was going on nobody noticed that the guy stole the code to the safe. He shared this info with me and offered co-op.
- Why didn't he want to go through with it on his own?
- He had plenty of cash but wanted to help me get back for my lost money. So we bought a house and I changed my name. We also searched for my "father" who was just some homeless bum willing to play the role in return for shelter and a bottle of beer from time to time. When I met you, my dearest Andrzej, you messed up my plans. After sometime I realized I loved you and asked you for help, remember?

Andrzej nodded.
- This is when you took care of those passports. I knew I could count on you.
- So, my little Kasia was doing all of this in revenge.
- Yes, it was all about the revenge. – She replied firmly.
- Who arranged the accident and, of course, the victim?
- That dude from Hollywood.
- All this sounds incredible. The guy has the code to the safe, fixes up a victim, robs the bank and shares the

profit with you. This had to be some idiot!!

- Hiis days were counted. E had AIDS. The girl he burnt in his car was his fiancée. He passed AIDS on her too, but unintentionally. He couldn't forgive himself this. When she died he didn't burry her but wanted to use her death to open a new life for me.
- Incredible story. You know, you also can lie like reading from notes.
- Bt I'll never be as good as you. Overall the idea of the accident on the lake was yours.

Andrzej got quiet. His face no longer carried a smile.

- I feel bad for Mark. He thinks I'm dead.
- That's why you should remember Poland. Some day we can arrange something to meet your brother there.
- You're right. This is a very good idea.

He regained energy again and smile reappeared on his face.

- Good, old Poland. Like a mother she watches over our actions. And when we get tired, and go back there after years, she welcomes us with open arms. Everybody back there is jealous of us living in the States or that we sunbathe under the Argentinean sun. Life in Poland or as an immigrant somewhere is no different. We have the same problems, we worry about our kids,

288

we don't want to lose our jobs, we
pay the bills. We make love to our
women and go to church.
- We steal out of anger. – Kasia added
and Andrzej busted out laughing.
- Yes, out of anger and once we pass
that out of greed.
This time Kasia also felt the wave of good
mood.
- And once we had our fun with the
money we tell everyone we drowned.
– She said laughing. Andrzej did too
and after a while said:
- Kasia Pitar from Sosnowiec robbed
an American banker, ha, ha, ha…
Kasia didn't quit.
- He drowned, the Polish
NIEOKRZESANY moron, was it a
magician swimming in the stormy
waves? No, it was Mr. Polskowicz,
ha, ha, ha – She kept laughing, tears
started dripping off her cheeks. They
laughed so loud all the birds walking
around the palm tree flew away.
Andrzej embraced Kasia and she
passionately held on to his neck.
- It's nice to reminisce the homeland. –
He said.
- It is, my dear, for sure.

In north western part of metro Detroit there is
a city of Southfield. At first glance it is just
one of thousands of small towns spread
around the U.S. But there is a thing that
makes Southfield very popular in the entire
area and it is the amount of law practices, the

base for local economy. They are like a magnet for the many people from various part of the country. "Town Center" is a complex of six skyscrapers. With exception of one hotel and one apartment building the rest belongs to businesses, half of which are law offices.

Mark walked into the hotel-skyscraper. Black windows of enormous sizes were cut with gold stripes placed on the concrete construction. The visual effect was great. Mark, however, didn't pay much attention to this. Years spent on doing business made him used to law offices. He walked into the elevator and pushed the button "30". The elevator took off.

"Yes, I have never ever thought it would come to me getting a divorce".

- Hi Mark. I was waiting for you. How is it going?
- All right.
- You want something to drink?
- No. Let's just get down to business. That's what I'm paying you for after all.
- Ok, ok. – The man said with a smile.

They walked into a large room. Windows had great view of the city. Marble floors and window gave the place a very formal and elegant look.

- Wow, Jerry. I see you're doing better and better. – Mark said.
- Well, it's not us who invite the people. They come here anyway on their own..

- OK, ok. When I hear your tone of voice and the stories about business I right away start feeling sorry for you.
- But that's the truth. I work hard and still there is no money.
- Oh stop lying. I
- I've known you for seven years and always hear the same story.
- I have to repeat it so that I don't forget how to complain.
- Ok, what's my situation like?
- You and your wife can each get half of what you have. Children are adults almost but for as long as they're in school you have to support them.
- Let's just do this. Give my wife everything; house, car, furniture. I will help her until she gets on her feet. I've supported my kids for seventeen years; I may as well keep on doing this.
- So why are you hiring me? You can get it all settled with your wife.
- She hired a lawyer so it's only appropriate that I'm represented properly too.
- Oh those divorces. Why do you want a divorce to begin with?
- I don't know myself. I guess that's my character. I constantly seek new adventures. I like starting everything anew. It strengthens me inside. I like creating situations, sometimes complicated ones but once everything turns out ok my satisfaction is just great.

- And if it turns bad?
- Then you draw conclusions, which you will use n the future.
- Why taking chances? You have enough experience with this business and with life.
- I can't help it. I'm free, I always have been and I will be. That's why I don't want to hurt those who are dear to me.
- But marriage should not be an obstacle for your plans.
- That's what everyone thinks. But after the years you have to review all of your marital agreements. You let your wife do things that you would never let her do in the past. And vice versa, she gives you a free hand. Third parties appear. The situation forces us to lie. Everybody knows about it but nobody is saying anything. It's a silent approval. This way we construct fictitious life harmony. This life, almost a forced one, is a torment. I prefer to tell the truth and leave than keep lying for the rest of my days.
- What about the children? – Jerry kept asking.
- They're mine and will be mine. Me not living with them changes absolutely nothing about my attitude towards them. Quite the opposite, maybe they'll see that there is life without dad who so far tried to fix all

of their problems. Maybe they'll pay more attention to their mother who also needs help. Maybe finally they will also start taking care of themselves; go back to school, quit the nightlife and drugs.

- I know what you mean. I have the same problems with my kids.
- Times change, people don't. Look Jerry, at the twentieth century: the first world war, Bolsheviks Revolution, the second world war, Hiroshima and Nagasaki, Hitler, Stalin communist empire, the Beatles and the man on the Moon, Korea, Vietnam, Peace Prizes, Afghanistan and Falklands, the great Olympic Games, the terrorist attacks, the Great America, and the diseases: cancer, AIDS, the failure of communism, Solidarity, Berlin Wall and now again the Persian Gulf...
- Stop it already. You made me tired. Al this will change, the economy will rid the thoughts about war. New technologies will allow the unheard of communication between people. The world will be open for everyone.
- Is this really what we want though? Look at the immigrants; most of them came here just to make some bucks. They could care less where would they live; California or New York, Texas or Montana, as long as the "greens" are in their hand.

- But that I the beauty of America - strong economy and democracy.
- And where is the love of the country? I guarantee you, Jerry, that if you unloaded all these dollars on Antarctica, the cold, inhabited land would become the oasis of the world.
- What is wrong with you today? Do you want to change the system or what?
- No, I don't want to change anything. These are just my observations.
- I'm sorry now, but I have to say goodbye to you. I have another client waiting already.
- Well, so when will all this be over?
- I will prepare the documents according to your wishes. Then we'll have a hearing in court.

Jerry paused for a second, thought and said:
- I think two weeks and it'll be all behind us.

Sport Mitsubishi "Eclipse" drove smooth on the road. Janek slowly turned to the side street.
- Are you sure you want to go to Ewelina's? – He asked his sister.
- Yes. – Ania answered. – It is getting late and I don't feel like taking another trip somewhere else yet. I'll call mom and tell her I'll spend a night here.
- We'll drive around the city for a while yet. – Janek said pointing at the

Black man sitting next to him. Ania
said:

- You better go home. First of all it's
not your car and besides you have to
be home by midnight. That's what
the judge said.
- Don't worry about me. Am I right? –
He asked the Black friend.
- For sure man. We're the best. Peace
on Earth.
- Dad will be mad. – Ania tried to
convince him once more.
- Our dad left us so it's not his business
ho we spend our time. Plus he took
my car away.
- But you stole his money.
- I didn't steal. I borrowed.
- Did you at least apologize?
- Not yet. But for what anyway? For
him taking away my car? Come on
man – he said to the guy – tell me, am
I right?
- Sure thing. We're the best. Peace on
Earth. – The Black kid spoke
gesticulating with his hand.

Janek pulled over in front of one of the
houses. Ania walked out and kissed her
brother goodnight.

- I'll see you tomorrow.
- See ya. – Janek answered.

The door shot. The car took off with an
impetus. The boys drove listening to rap
music. After a while they passed by the nice,
well taken care off neighborhoods and drove
into the ghetto; dark streets, burnt down
houses, dirty prostitutes walking around. At

the end of one of the streets there was a building. From far a distance it looked like a warehouse or something. During the day it probably did fulfill the role of a major storage facility, but during the Saturday nights it was an oasis for the rich kids hungry for excitement.

Rage Party – this is how it was commonly referred to meant simply a really rough and brutal private party. Drunk kids walk around the large hall looking for new forms of this idiotic fun. Drugs are everywhere. Sexual orgies cannot satisfy even the most animalistic instincts of people who are totally high and drunk. The music is most likely just the echo of what's going on in brains of the kids. What's the trill? Hard to say. They won't remember it tomorrow anyway.

- Hi guys! – Someone yelled in direction of Janek and his buddy. – Want some more booze?
- Nah, that's enough. I'm driving. – Janek tried to refuse.
- How about some ecstasy, just to chill out?
- Give me some. – Janek's Black friend said.
- Here you are.

While Ryan was getting drugged up, Janek looked around.

- What a mess. – He thought. – Dirt and stench. Half naked chicks don't even resemble humans. What an idiot I am to spend here the cash that would cover my car payment.

Ryan interrupted his thinking.

- What's up Janek. No fear. We're the best. Peace on earth.

Janek grabbed him by the hand and took to the parking lot.

- We're going. – He said. – I have to be home by midnight by the court order.
- Fuck the court order. – Ryan started to mumble.
- Maybe that's what you think, but I have a different view on that.
- We're going back inside. We'll get some girls. – Ryan mumbled even worse but Janek did not feel like getting into some debate. He pushed his friend inside the car and thought: "I'm going back to my hockey buddies. Life was much smoother around them plus dad would be happy". He himself sat in the car and turned the engine on.
- No fear, my man. – Ryan started to repeat himself but more and more inoherently.
- Would you please shut up? – Janek was getting mad. Ryan didn't answer, just rocked to the rhythm of the music.
- Turn this down! – Janek demanded. Ryan looked at him surprised.
- Since when do you mind?
- This is nothing but noise and cursing.

Ryan didn't react, just sat there peacefully and kept on rocking. After a while though said:

- Janek, pull over. I have to puke.

-   You can't stop on this part of the
    road. – Janek answered. – I will turn
    into the next side street.
-   No, pull over now!

Janek wasn't answering. He looked for place
to stop. At some point Ryan suddenly shook
like he was shot or something. He grabbed
the steering wheel and directed it to the right.
The car reacted instantly. Janek lost control.
He tried to slam the brakes. "Bang!" - they
hit the building on the corner of the road…

Mare sat alone in his new house. After the
divorce he liked to spend sometime thinking
about things. He stared at the desk: photos
of Janek, Ania and Andrzej reminded him of
the times spent together.
"I wanted to do so much for you – he thought
looking at the photos of his son – Now all
there's left is to visit your gave.   And where
are you? – now he looked at the photo of his
brother. – I don't even know if you're alive".
He walked up to the cabinet, took a glass and
the bottle of cognac. Golden drink poured
into the oval glass. He lit up a cigarette and
sat again at the desk, pushed a button and the
computer screen lit up with its silver color.
All there was left to listen to was the sound
of buttons pushed. Letters appeared on the
screen and soon the words "The Twenty First
Century" evolved. Mark looked at the screen
and smiled.
"I will write a poem. I have to be myself
again. I can't bee just the money making
machine". He took a big drag and sipped on

his cognac. His fingers started to travel
around the keyboard very fast…

"There will those who read these words
Who will consider me a heretic.
But I want to tell you about a land,
Whose name America is.
On my way here
I had my ways, I had my views
And so I was nice and kind
Waiting for the problems to end.
As it often happens in life
This theory was false.
I worked quite hard, along with my bro
In the midst of my trying I simply forgot
That money doesn't rule.
Andrzej would say: "Don't work just know
How to go about the things in this world".
And so I learned this and I did succeed,
And I could afford doing as I pleased.
I shot some golf, I drank some booze
But always stayed for others up for use.
"What a guy you are" – the boys would
always say.
"To learn the street smart rules, is a hard
work too".
And so I fell in love with this life of mine
But only till I looked into my childern's
mind.
The school no longer mattered; another party
waited,
And the thrill of staying up all night would
not be even debated.
Once I tried the spanking to bit some wisdom
in them

The government yelled at me, and came with
the smart defense;
"Don't you ever dare, arguing with your
kids"
I wanted to say something, but figured out
keep quiet
How lucky I felt not to go to jail!
The problem, however, bothers me at times:
Why the Polish children want to pass for
Black?
They listen to rap music, dressed strangely
too,
Once you say name "Poland", they will ask
you "Who?"
So don't bother searching, better learn to lie,
The government will raise them, since it
knows best how.
And so I believed this; they know better, true.
Overall who am I: a wild Pole like you.
I left the kids alone, took up politics;
White House in the background, large
orchestra plays tunes.
And I'm just looking there, there at the
screen
I see the president speak – surely words of
wit.
Well, I was wrong again, dear friend of mine,
No word on poverty, not even the missiles,
He talked about women – what a surprise!
"I did that one already, this one bores me by
now
Monika was a sweetheart but I just let her
blow".
I watched the show and was shocked, to be
true,

What president, what government run lives of
me and you?
I still didn't say a word,
Us, Poles are humble.
I now took up the issues of economy.
There's three hundred million of us, living
here in U.S.
Everybody's smiling, everybody's happy.
And how much do we owe – this we
wouldn't say.
Dad, mom and children – they all work too
hard.
"They want to better themselves".
Oh, no! They just want to buy of the debt.
Not just one beautiful mind, figured it out by
now,
Like it or not, here everybody owes.
Why worry, the government remembers,
Oops, excuse the mistake – itself it has not a
single cent.
So how does it work, that the whole nation
works,
And whatever they make they use to buy
their debts off.
And where does this come from – the money,
the strange,
Which satisfies each and every wish.
The government says: "We just don't have
it".
People keep whining,
Must be the Angels and God doing the
printing.
I keep on thinking and have to admit,
I no longer believe in economy either.
When a man is worth only the sum he pays
off,

This is why the poor don't count, just and
only rich.
Too much of my mind is occupied by dough
though,
So let me touch a bit on the international
ground.
Everybody thought, once the WWII ends,
That the peace would finally become a
permanent guest.
Jews in Israel rejoice, for they didn't have to
wander,
But what happened next?
The war was just about to begin.
Those in great Russia, on the other hand,
Simply don't care.
Whoever rules: capitalists or Bolsheviks.
Only here, poor Americans
Send the planes upon request.
They shoot here, they bomb there,
At the end, it will all be added to the common
debt.
Finally in Europe, where things start to go
bad,
A popular news got its wings and spread.
Why argue, why confront, since we can all
work together
And so the decided to make all countries
brothers.
One problem only:
Who will be payin?
Why would United Europe bother with this
detail?
Let' write to God, he'll print us some more.
Well, Poland is different, not like ages ago.
Now the Germans and French and Brits are
our friends.

Whatever possible, they will buy in Poland.
But they want accept us as part of their own.
It is hard for us to get rich in Poland,
What will happen when finally the time
comes
To pay debt in the United Europe?
In America, we're not trouble-free either.
Each day we have to be mindful of the rest of
the world,
Whom to give some? Whom to take away
from? And whom to loan?
Nobody has just simply given yet for
nothing.
An average Joe worked and will always
work.
It's so much easier to get wealthy, yes.
But it's also hard to pay off all debt.
So don't be fooled my dear country man
from Poland
That it is so easy to live here.
You want to know the truth?
I'll tell a secret, that sometimes it's better
back there.
And don't look at me, an old romantic type,
Who will point out your errors.
In truth there isn't anything new in this world
And we already are in the twenty first
century.

He finished writing. Stood up from his desk,
put the shoes on and walked out on the street.
Slowly he came up to his mailbox and looked
inside.
"Junk mail again" – he thought to himself. In
between colorful advertisings he spotted a
letter. He took the envelope and looked at

the place where address was supposed to be. But instead of the name only one word was written: "Pinto".

"Is this some joke" – he thought and wanted to throw the letter to trash. But something stopped him.

"Pinto, Pinto – only Andrzej and Angela knew about the dog, my L.A. friend", he opened the letter nervous and began to read: "I'm sorry Mark for everything I've done. I did not want to mail this letter via regular mail that's why I passed through a friend to put into your mailbox. Love knows no boundaries and we never know what will provoke us. Angela hasn't died. She's alive. I will tell you also that she is Polish. She talked some guy in L.A. into robbing a bank and it worked but she had to disappear. I had to do the same so that the cops couldn't trace her. We live in Buenos Aires. We're doing good. I can't tell you what names we use. From four hundred thousand she "made", we've only lost one hundred thousand and the rest was given away to charity. Her real name is Kasia and likely we'll get married soon. I have to see you. Let's meet in Poland, in the same place where we slept during our last high school vacation before we found a spot on the camping site. I'll be waiting there for you on June 9, 2002. Take care of yourself – you moron, and don't let get manipulated.

I don't have to remind you that all this is just between you and I. Give the kids kisses and Aneta too, but don't tell them it's from me". Andrzej.

Mark placed the letter in his pocket and walked back inside the house.

- He's alive! – He screamed. Then he started to think: "He gave three hundred thousand to charity. Now, that I don't believe".
- He's alive! – He screamed again.

He walked quickly to his desk and looked for something for a while. He pulled out a piece of paper with the telephone number to agent Johnson with the FBI. He looked at it and tore it up.

"To you he'll be dead forever", he thought. He poured himself another glass of cognac, sat in the armchair and turned the tape recorder on. The lyrics of the song and the smell of flowers put him in excellent mood. He sang along with the tape:

"Thought walk out of the shadow, something changes inside of the man and he comes back from his journey, to the sunny land".

www.ingramcontent.com/pod-product-compliance
Lightning Source LLC
Chambersburg PA
CBHW070755280626
47162CB00016B/569